Alan Hunter was born in Hoveton, Norfolk, in 1922. He left school at the age of fourteen to work on his father's farm, spending his spare time sailing on the Norfolk Broads and writing nature notes for the *Eastern Evening News*. He also wrote poetry, some of which was published while he was in the RAF during the Second World War. By 1950, he was running his own bookshop in Norwich. In 1955, the first of what would become a series of forty-six George Gently novels was published. He died in 2005, aged eighty-two.

110654804

The Inspector George Gently series

Gently at a Gallop

Alan Hunter

ROBINSON

Constable & Robinson Ltd.
55–56 Russell Square
London WC1B 4HP
www.constablerobinson.com

First published in the UK by Cassell & Company Ltd., 1971

This paperback edition published by Robinson,
an imprint of Constable & Robinson Ltd., 2013

Copyright © Alan Hunter 1971

The right of Alan Hunter to be identified as the
author of this work has been asserted by him in accordance
with the Copyright, Designs & Patents Act 1988

This is a work of fiction. Names, characters, places and incidents are either
the product of the author's imagination or are used fictitiously, and any
resemblance to actual persons, living or dead, or to actual events or
locales is entirely coincidental

All rights reserved. This book is sold subject to the condition
that it shall not, by way of trade or otherwise, be lent, re-sold,
hired out or otherwise circulated in any form of binding or cover
other than that in which it is published and without a similar condition
including this condition being imposed on the subsequent purchaser.

A copy of the British Library Cataloguing in Publication
Data is available from the British Library

ISBN 978-1-78033-946-7 (paperback)
ISBN 978-1-47210-464-9 (ebook)

Typeset by TW Typesetting, Plymouth, Devon

Printed and bound by CPI Group (UK) Ltd, Croydon, CR0 4YY

3 5 7 9 10 8 6 4 2

CHAPTER ONE

S EAWARDS THE SUN was burning off the mist, but as yet it still clung to the high plateau of the heath. The thick bush-heather was sodden with moisture and scoured Cator's stout boots as he stumbled through it. It was August, and the heather was flowering, but in the mist it was dark and drab: more colourful were the yellow tabs of the gorse, which grew in low, scanty islands.

The heath was silent. It had little bird-life. Cator had rarely seen a snake or a lizard. Between the continents of ling and bell heather ran trackways of stones and growthless grey sand. The slanted plane of the heath was fretted with valleys and frequent ridges and hollows. Towards the sea it cut off sharply in precipitous falls, bushed and pathless.

Cator reached the mouth of one of the valleys which drove upwards to the summit of the heath. Its sides were shaggy with shoulder-high bracken in which tints of russet had begun to show. To his left, above a hard skyline, a pale disc of sun swam in the vapour; for brief seconds it warmed the valley with a surge of colour, then chilled and faded in fresh wrack.

Cator plodded on. Up the valley ran a track, but it was narrow and impeded by the wiry heather. Once, where it crossed a burn of sand, he checked his stride, seeing there the print of a horse's hoof. A recent print . . . ? Cator couldn't be certain. Not many riders ventured this way. He planted his boot on the half-moon, leaving in its place a pattern of nails.

Now he was half-way up the valley and approaching its solitary landmark. This was a ragged thicket of hawthorn and bramble, drooping down the right-hand slope. Nearing it, Cator paused again. He had noticed an object at the foot of the hawthorns. Dark and still, it resembled a small heap of wet, discarded clothing. Somebody lying there? That seemed unlikely, in the early-morning mist. Cator's breath came faster. He began to lope forward, careless of the heather that soaked his ankles. He reached the hawthorns. He saw death. Cator wasn't afraid of death. A farm-worker, he was familiar with the stiffened carrion of dead animals. The animal here was a man-animal, but Cator saw it without shock: he stood staring, breathing through his teeth, trying to understand what he saw.

The body was male; it was wet; it was stiff; it had received damage. It lay on its back with one arm thrown up and the other evidently fractured, and the hand crushed. One leg also was apparently fractured and the chest had a curious, sunken appearance. The features were partly pulped and they retained a semicircular impression in the broken flesh. Around the body were signs of disorder. Cator noticed scuff-marks in the sand. An area of heather-bush had been churned up and several of the embedded flints were kicked out.

Though he'd never met such a thing before, Cator could guess what he was looking at: this man had been savaged by a horse. It had left its signature in his face.

Cator felt horror. He took some steps backwards, when suddenly the sun broke through behind him. It lit the dank side of the valley and coloured the mist still heaped above it. And on the mist, printed high and clear, was the rainbow shadow of a gigantic horseman, sitting motionless, his horse still, his face turned, watching Cator. It was the illusion of a moment; then the mist closed again. The rasp of Cator's breathing had been the only sound to accompany the phantasm.

Cator ran. He dashed up the valley, his legs pumping like machines, boots squeaking in the heather, arms thrashing the moist air.

On a ridge behind him sat the horseman whose presence had occasioned the phenomenon.

He was dressed in black, and rode a black horse.

He chuckled, watching Cator run.

'Does the name Lachlan Stogumber mean anything to you?' the Assistant Commissioner (Crime) asked Gently.

Gently considered it, making at the same time a swift mental review of the morning papers.

'Is he a pop singer?' he ventured.

'Not a pop singer,' said the A.C.

'Does he play for Spurs?'

'He isn't a footballer. At least, I wouldn't think it likely.'

'Well . . . a Black Power leader?'

The A.C. grinned. 'Admit it,' he said. 'You don't know him. The man Stogumber has made no mark in your nasty, criminous little sub-world.'

3

Gently rocked his shoulders. 'My loss,' he said. 'So who is Stogumber – among the elect?'

'The elect,' the A.C. said, 'being the pot-smoking stratum and presumably the editor of the *New Statesman*. He's a poet.'

'Stogumber is a poet?'

'According to the authorities quoted. He's the young Byron of the jazz idiom. Allow me to make an introduction.'

The A.C. picked a copy of the *New Statesman* from his in-tray and folded it back at a marked page. Gently accepted it without enthusiasm; a culture session was not among his priorities. The Assistant Commissioner, it was as well to know, had himself published verse when at Cambridge: he had been a near-contemporary of Auden and Spender, and rather viewed himself as leaguing with them. The politic didn't lightly enter upon these topics with the A.C.

'Read it,' the A.C. said. 'Give me an opinion.'

Gently fidgeted. 'This isn't my century. I'm a little Après-Keats-le-déluge.'

'So try reading Stogumber,' the A.C. said.

Gently sighed, and tried reading Stogumber. Stogumber was less enigmatic than Gently had feared. His title, *A Mood A*, was not explicit, but the words that followed had a wistful coherence.

Mood a mood a mood   not
strictly a mood neither
dumskull   but
brainumbra   mind dreaming   mind
diffuse   loitering   seeing   floating

4

that's
me   nothing/everything   me
escaped   seeking bars   seeking
creation: damnably free

Scribbling ideas strictly nonviable   forcing
words strictly styleless   separated
at least a century from
the old versemaker   (me?

Hallo down there in the dark   gnome
mining in chaos   old
mole   what have you found   what
tidings from Hades?

Here's a lost soul listening in
the hours his ears   shout it out   shout
shout

(Or whisper my love   he'll hear

Gently cleared his throat. 'Interesting,' he said. 'It could be a code, but probably isn't.'

'There you go,' the A.C. said. 'I think Stogumber has passion. I'm not sure that I'm sympathetic with his excursions into punctuation, but I like his energy, and the shrewd picture of a creator stuck for a subject. Brainumbra – rather fine.'

'Yes,' Gently said. 'But what's he to us?'

'I'm coming to it,' the A.C. said. 'Briefly, Lachlan Stogumber had a brother-in-law called Charles Berney – a brewer.'

'A brewer,' Gently said. 'Berney's Fine Ales and Stout?'

'They're the people. They were taken over by Watney's in a reshuffle a few months back. Berney was given a seat on the new board and the usual office and pseudo-job, very pleasant. It left him free to pursue what was apparently the hobby of a lifetime.'

'But Berney is dead?'

The A.C. nodded. 'He died on Tuesday. He was trampled by a horse.'

'So what is our interest?'

'Just that. The Mid-Northshire Police are uneasy.'

Gently stared blankly. 'But it's an Act of God – being trampled by a horse!'

The A.C. nodded sympathetically. 'And a ruling you would expect to appeal to constabularies in the remoter provinces. Brewer stricken by Act of God. Divine judgement on Berney's Fine Ales. It must be all this box-culture that's destroying the simple faith.' He rubbed his chin. 'Berney was a womanizer. That was the hobby I mentioned. He appears to have been keeping an assignation when he got mixed up with the horse.'

'What's the woman's story?'

'She hasn't been identified.'

'Who owns the horse?'

'They haven't found it.'

'So,' Gently said. 'No horse. No woman. Just a brewer dead from injuries. Why couldn't he have been knocked down by a bus?'

'Because it happened on a heath,' the A.C. said.

The A.C. graciously ordered coffee, which was fetched by a policewoman of elegant statistics. The A.C. drank his coffee waspishly, like a man remembering cigarettes.

'Of course, Mid-Northshire may have made a cock-up and offended some people round there. Berney could have been savaged by a stray. You wouldn't expect the owner to come forward. Then the local Keystones move in demanding alibis and insinuating adultery. Last resort: call the Yard, try to make it look real.'

'Is that how you read it?' Gently asked.

'Smoke if you damn well have to,' the A.C. said. He licked his lips and put down his cup. 'It gives me that impression,' he admitted. 'Berney was a womanizer – fact: but they have no evidence of a current affair. And against that he remarried only three months ago. You'd think he'd still be resting on his laurels.'

'Perhaps his carefree past caught up with him,' Gently suggested.

'Blackmail?'

'Berney would have money.'

'Why kill him then?'

Gently shrugged. He began to fill his pipe with Erinmore.

'Berney was forty-five,' the A.C. said. 'He gave a birthday party on Monday. Acting normally, you'd say, showing no signs of strain. But next morning he told his wife he had to attend a directors' meeting in London, which involved staying overnight. And that was a lie. There wasn't a meeting.'

'The classic storyline,' Gently said.

'Yes, well,' the A.C. said. 'But what he actually did was to drive to Starmouth and book a single room in the name of Timson. Note, a single room. No suggestion of a Mrs Timson to follow.'

'Perhaps she was already there.'

'Then Berney would still be alive.'

Gently puffed. The A.C. made an impulsive fanning motion.

'And that's it – we lose sight of him after he booked at the Britannic at Starmouth. He left in his car at around ten a.m. and some time after that drove to High Hale heath. His stomach contents say he ate a picnic lunch, and there was an empty Thermos flask in the car. He died around four p.m., about a mile from the car, on a remote part of the heath. He wasn't expected home, so no alarm. A farm-worker found him on Wednesday morning.'

'And a horse did it – and that's all they have?'

'There isn't much else,' the A.C. said. 'They have a witness who saw a horseman on the heath Tuesday afternoon, but too far off for identification. Apparently there's a riding school three miles away, and they occasionally take riders to High Hale heath. But nothing on Tuesday. The only horse on the spot belongs to a farmer, and that's accounted for.'

Gently puffed. 'Then was it a horse?'

The A.C. hesitated. 'They seemed pretty sure of it.'

'You could run a man down, dump him on a heath, plant a few horseshoe marks around him.'

The A.C. stared a moment, then shook his head. 'I don't think you could get away with that trick. Vehicle-collision injuries are too distinctive. It would need more than faked hoofmarks to pull it off. And don't forget the horseman.'

'I wasn't forgetting him. Somebody saw him a great way off.'

'He was there,' the A.C. said. 'That's the point. If his

presence was innocent, you'd have thought he'd have come forward.'

'Huh,' Gently said. He brooded a little. 'Where did Berney live?' he asked.

'At High Hale Lodge.'

'Is that near the heath?'

'I don't have that information,' the A.C. said.

Gently blew a lop-sided smoke-ring. 'So Berney takes a day off,' he said. 'He's expecting it to be a night off, too, and he books a room, name of Timson. His wife thinks he's gone to London, but as far as we know he didn't leave the district. It reads as though he drove straight back to High Hale, parked, then waited to keep an afternoon rendezvous. Was the car concealed?'

'Yes,' the A.C. said. 'It was driven on the heath and parked out of sight.'

'Just making points,' Gently said. 'But why did Berney wait about there so long?'

The A.C. frowned. 'We don't know that he did. There's no evidence that he drove straight back.'

'There's the picnic lunch.'

'Perhaps he thought he was safest there. Driving about, he might have been spotted.'

Gently nodded reluctantly. 'We'll pass that for the present. Berney eats his sandwiches, drinks his coffee. Now, the theory is, he sets off across the heath to a spot a mile distant, to meet a woman. Why so far?'

'Perhaps handy for her.'

'Couldn't he have parked somewhere closer?'

The A.C. gestured with his hand. 'This is all academic! No doubt it'll be plain enough when you've seen the layout.'

'What keeps striking me,' Gently said, 'is that Berney went to these lengths just to meet a woman. We aren't dealing with calf-love. Berney was forty-five with, we are told, a long history of philandering. Would this be his style? Wouldn't you rather have expected him to have made that room at Starmouth a double?'

'It seems more his mark,' the A.C. agreed. 'But we don't know the circumstances. What are you suggesting?'

Gently shrugged. 'Points,' he said. 'Checking to see if the theory fits.'

He put another match to his pipe, kindly puffing the smoke aside. The A.C. twitched a little but refrained from stronger reaction.

'Berney meets his woman, then, and while they're dallying they're being watched by the aggrieved husband. The husband is mounted; is, we assume, the horseman seen by the witness. The woman departs. Berney heads for his car. The husband follows Berney and rides him down. Husband rides home, stables horse, declares an alibi. Wife supports him.'

'Well?' the A.C. asked sourly.

'It's half-way credible,' Gently admitted. 'The wife would be scared of the husband and would probably feel she was responsible. But the locals haven't come up with a woman and they haven't come up with a horse.'

'Which,' the A.C. said, 'is where we came in. Go down there and find them for them, Gently.'

Gently sighed and rose.

'Any message for Lachlan Stogumber?' he asked.

'Tell him to use aspirin,' the A.C. said. He was reaching for an aerosol as Gently left.

* * *

There was mist again on the heath, lying low and smoky in valleys and hollows. The western sky held a tender pink afterglow banded by still, heliotrope clouds. The cool plain of the sea below took a tinge of the pink in its slaty flood. Overhead a few stars prickled. No scent came from the dank heather.

A man was seated on one of the ridges and he had binoculars slung round his neck. He sat as still as the stunted thorn-bushes that grew in a screen about him. He watched and listened. Suddenly, quietly, he raised the binoculars to his eyes. For a long while he remained staring through them, motionless, forearms supported on his knees. Then he lowered them, but continued to sit there, the damp twilight thickening round him. At last he heard a sound, a long way off: the sound of a car engine being started.

Then the man rose, getting up stiffly in a way that showed he was no longer young. But he was tall and strongly framed; very silent in all his movements.

CHAPTER TWO

Hot, plodding, august sun blazoned the main street of Low Hale as the white Lotus Plus 2 drifted in from the Norchester Road. It was nearing noon, and very warm. Heat was shimmering above parked cars. Men and women in light summer clothes lingered in the shade of the shop canopies. The Lotus crept through very slowly, as though even it were feeling the heat. Its driver, pipe in mouth, peered curiously at the period fronts, the small family shops. Plaster, brick, faced flint, pantiles kiln-hot in the sun: a haphazard place, built in haphazard styles. Half-way along, the Royal William jutted out into the traffic. A big, white-plastered hotel, it carried a Berney's Fine Ales sign. The Lotus paused there and seemed likely to park where, even in Low Hale, parking would have been naughty; but then it slid on again, silk-smooth, a white fish in the sun-struck street.

At the town's end, off the coast road, stood a large, stodgy building of Fletton brick. It was shaded by limes and cars were parked before it; the white Lotus joined these.

* * *

'First . . . a drink!'

The ops-room at Low Hale, though dimmed with blinds, was close and ovenish. Coming into it, Gently had begun to sweat as he hadn't sweated in the moving car.

Five men were waiting for him there: the sharp-faced district Chief Super, Banham; Docking, the C.I.D. Inspector i/c; his Sergeant, Bayfield; and a couple of D.C.s. A reception committee – and Gently had been gracious, shaking hands all round. But now – first things first. What he needed was a beer.

'Will a lager do you?'

'Two lagers will.'

Banham smiled politely and signalled to one of the D.C.s.

'You found it warm coming along, did you?'

'Yes. It's a race day at Newmarket.'

Banham whistled sympathy through his teeth. He was a large man, wearing a tight uniform.

They sat down round the desk, leaving the chair behind it for Gently. Docking, tow-haired, earnest-featured, was nursing a fat green file. The lager came: Gently swallowed his first glass in silence, then refilled the glass and set it down on the desk. He looked his audience over.

'Right,' he said. 'Some facts about Berney to kick off with.'

They stirred a little. Banham looked at Docking.

'Well, he was a right bastard, sir,' Docking began.

'With the women.'

'Yes, sir, the women. Didn't seem able to keep his

hands off them. He was paying a couple of maintenance orders, and there were scandals all over the place.'

'Tell me about them.'

Docking hitched at his file. 'There was his first wife for a start, sir,' he said. 'She'd been married to Laing, Berney's solicitor, but Laing divorced her, naming Berney.'

'Then she turned round and divorced Berney,' Banham chuckled.

'Yes, sir,' Docking said. 'Their marriage didn't last long. Berney was named in another suit, and his first wife petitioned, using that as grounds.'

'How long ago?' Gently asked.

Docking dived into the file. 'Nineteen-sixty.'

'But he's been named once or twice since then,' Banham said. 'And we've heard of a few cases that didn't end in court. There was one last year, a fellow called Norman – it's down in the book as a Domestic Dispute. Norman pasted the daylights out of Berney, but when we got there, Berney wouldn't complain.'

'Where was Norman on Tuesday?'

Banham looked at Docking.

'He's on holiday in Spain, sir,' Docking said.

'Go on, then,' Gently said, sipping. 'What else have we got that's up to date?'

Docking had the file open again. 'I've a list of five here, sir. Of course, you realize, sir, it's based on gossip. It's not the sort of thing we can . . . well, verify.'

'Understood,' Gently said.

'There's Mrs Pleasants,' Docking said. 'She's the doctor's wife, High Hale village. She's been seen in Berney's car. Mrs Drury, she's the wife of Arthur Drury, the auctioneer. Mrs Wade, her husband is Town Clerk here in Low Hale. Mrs Jefferies, the Jefferies run a guest-house at Clayfield. And Mrs Amies, her husband is the secretary of Gorsehills Golf Club. According to our information, these have all been seen in Berney's company in the past eighteen months.'

'Sounds formidable,' Gently said. 'And a marriage and maintenance orders thrown in.'

'I'd say he was a bit of a nutter,' Banham put in. 'The devil, you don't *need* that number of women.'

'Perhaps he was trying to prove something, sir,' Docking suggested. 'Scared about his potency, something like that.'

'It's the women who ought to have been scared,' Banham said. 'Yet they always fall for this kind of a nutter.'

Gently sipped more lager. 'You'll have checked on the husbands?'

'We've reports on all five,' Docking said. 'The doctor was out on his rounds that afternoon, but the rest were at their places of work.'

'How many own horses?'

'None, sir. But Drury and the Jefferies go riding.'

'Where?'

'Clayfield, sir. The Berneys also used to ride there.'

'It's about three miles from High Hale,' Banham explained. 'A couple called Rising run a stable there. Six or seven hacks and a string of ponies. That's where the people round here go to ride.'

'And of course, you've checked it.'

'First thing,' Banham said. 'I went over to Clayfield myself. But none of their horses was out on Tuesday,

15

there was just Mrs Rising teaching the children.' He passed his hand over his brow. 'Frankly, this is the problem,' he said. 'There aren't many horses near High Hale, and none of them were being ridden on Tuesday.'

Gently shrugged. 'Wasn't there one on a farm, somewhere?' Banham looked at Docking, who looked at Bayfield.

'The Home Farm, High Hale,' Bayfield said promptly. 'It's a stallion, belongs to the farmer, Nat Creke. Says it was in its loose-box all day, just went out for exercise in the evening. I think he was telling the truth, sir.'

'Then there's a gelding at the Old Rectory, sir,' Docking said. 'Belongs to a Mr Brooke, an accountant. It was in its paddock. Several people saw it.'

Gently nodded slowly. 'And that's the lot?'

'Unless someone fetched a horse in from elsewhere, sir.'

'And we're quite certain that a horse and nothing else killed Berney?'

Docking stared. Then he opened his file.

In effect, they'd called in a vet; but the photographs showed what little doubt there could have been. Berney's mangled body amongst the trampled heather evoked a frightful image of what had taken place. The horse had reared and come down on Berney, punching its hooves through flesh and bone; several times. Chest and skull were crushed, and a cruel trademark left in the face. Tantalizingly, this was the only hoofprint. The packed, gravelly soil showed nothing but scuff-marks. A report attached to the photographs revealed that a wide area had been searched with no better luck.

'Could you get a car to the spot?'

'Not into the valley, sir,' Docking said. 'You could perhaps get a Land-Rover somewhere near it.'

'Any signs of that?'

Docking shook his head.

So that was it. There had to be a horse – local or imported, they'd have to find him. Though it meant searching every shed and farm building in the district, and perhaps checking horses over half the county.

Gently finished the tepid remains of his second lager. 'Let's get back to Berney,' he said. 'If Berney was running true to form, then there's one person who'd probably know it. What does Mrs Berney tell us?'

'Not very much,' Banham said, mopping. 'I've had a couple of talks with the lady, and either she doesn't know or she's not saying. The way she tells it Berney had reformed, had never looked at another woman since he was married. It was all sweetness and light, with him having found the right woman at last.'

'How does she account for Berney's actions on Tuesday?'

'She just about called me a liar,' Banham said. 'She won't believe he booked a room in Starmouth, nor that he never intended going to London. Berney was hoaxed, that's her line. Somebody kidded him about the board meeting. Then, when somehow he tumbled to it, they lured him on to the heath and did him.'

Gently hesitated. 'He did book that room?'

'Yes. The manager of the Britannic knew Berney by sight. When he saw the paper he gave us a ring, and we collected "Timson's" case. It was Berney's.'

'Intriguing,' Gently said. He twirled his empty glass

for a moment. 'If Mrs Berney were only partly right, it might account for a point that's been puzzling me.'

'What point is that?' Banham asked.

'Berney's behaviour,' Gently said. 'It sticks out the more because of what you've been telling me – that Berney was a sure-fire, hell-bent womanizer. Yet here we have him making extravagant arrangements, driving miles, waiting for hours – and for what? He isn't even going to spend the night with this woman. At the most, he's going to roll her on the heath. He could have taken her in on his afternoon's stroll.'

Banham shifted uneasily, his chair creaking. 'Perhaps he couldn't shake off his missus.'

'Why not? He needed only to tell her he was going in to the office.'

'She might have checked, sir,' Docking said.

'She might have checked anyway,' Gently said. 'And if she did, a man of Berney's calibre would have had a ready lie. No, it doesn't add up. Berney had too much campaign experience. On top of which we have to remember he's only just married a young wife. What's she like?'

Banham wagged his shoulders. 'Attractive. Struck me as being quite a bomb. One thing, though.'

'What?'

'She's pregnant. It's been known to put a man off.'

Gently shrugged. 'All the same! Perhaps her ideas aren't so crazy. Berney may have lied to her about the board meeting, and still there needn't be a woman involved. If Berney was really in love with his wife then he'd be vulnerable to blackmail, and a blackmail threat makes a better motive for the way he behaved on Tuesday.'

Banham stared sweatily. One of the D.C.s murmured

to Docking. Docking dug into the file again and came up with a report sheet.

'About Berney's relations with his wife, sir.'

Gently flicked the glass. 'Well?'

'Detective Constable Lubbock had a chat with Mrs Haynes, who's the domestic help up at the Lodge. She was there on Monday evening, giving a hand with Berney's birthday party. She says that Berney had a letter, and that his wife snatched it from him.'

'Just like that?' Gently said.

'Sir,' D.C. Lubbock said, flushing. 'It was after the party, when the guests were gone. Mrs Haynes was collecting dirty glasses. The lounge door was ajar, and she glanced through it into the hall. She saw Berney reading a letter, then Mrs Berney grabbed it off him.'

'Was there a row?'

'No, sir. Berney just stood there looking foolish.'

'And this, of course, was a love-letter?'

D.C. Lubbock blushed silently.

Docking rustled the report sheet. '*I* reckoned it would be a love-letter, sir,' he said 'It seemed to make a bit of sense, knowing what we do about Berney. So then the lady would be lying when she says Berney'd finished with other women. And that makes sense too, sir – she wouldn't want to admit he was still at it.'

Gently flicked the glass again. It produced a sharp musical note. 'Still using sense,' he said. 'How do you reckon Berney came by that letter?'

'Sir?'

'The party is just over. Berney's been seeing off his guests. Then suddenly he has a letter.' Gently gave the glass another flick.

19

Docking's eyes rounded. 'One of the guests!'

'Have we a list of them?'

'Well . . . no.'

'I know of a couple,' Banham said quickly. 'Jerry Rising and his wife.'

'That's the man with the riding-stable?'

Banham nodded, dashing at his sweat.

'What's his wife like?'

'Pretty,' Banham said. 'And Berney used to go riding there.'

Gently sat broodingly for some moments, one finger still stroking the glass.

'All right,' he said at last. 'But let's not rush it. We don't even know that the letter was a love-letter.'

'But it fits,' Banham urged. 'Rising has horses. He's only three miles away, at Clayfield.'

'And he'd have opportunity, sir,' Docking put in. 'His wife was out with the children that day.'

Gently waved a hand. 'So we'll keep him in mind! But just at present it's still conjecture. Meanwhile, what we need is a complete list of guests – it may have some other interesting names on it.' He looked at Banham. 'Do we know of any more?'

'Only two of her people,' Banham said grumpily. 'Leonard Redmayne, that's her father's cousin, and of course, her brother. He's the poet.'

'Lachlan Stogumber?'

Banham looked surprised. 'I didn't think you'd have heard of him,' he said. 'I tried to read some of his stuff once. It didn't make much sense to me.'

Gently grinned. 'He's a famous man. Our Assistant

20

Commissioner knew about him. Who's Leonard Red-mayne?'

'He's the naturalist fellow. He lives with the family at the Manor.'

'And those are all you know about?'

Banham nodded. 'It didn't strike me to ask about the guests,' he said. 'It was a tricky business anyway, talking to the widow. Never knew when she'd burst into tears.'

Gently chivvied the glass a little more. 'Right,' he said. 'We're beginning to get the picture. A couple of other small points, then perhaps we can plan some action. Who was the witness who saw that horseman?'

'A Mrs Bircham,' Docking said. 'She's a pensioner. She has a cottage on the edge of the heath.'

'Any details?'

'Not really, sir. She thinks the horse was a dark colour. Says it was a long way off, on one of the ridges, not much more than a silhouette. She thinks she saw it at about a quarter to four, which fits the E.T.D. nicely.'

'Good,' Gently nodded. 'Second point. Who was the man who found the body?'

'Name of Cator,' Docking said. 'He works at High Noon Farm. He was crossing the heath to the village to pick up a bus there.'

'Does he work with horses?'

Docking shook his head. 'Cator's a tractor-driver,' he said. He hesitated. 'He was pretty shaken up when I saw him. Told me something I didn't put in the report.'

'What was that?'

'Says he saw a ghost.'

'A ghost!' Gently said. 'What sort of a ghost?'

21

'The ghost of a horseman,' Docking said. 'A big 'un. Up in the mist above the body.'

Gently paused. 'Was there a mist that morning?'

'It was thick early on,' Docking said. 'Then the sun broke it up. It was clear enough when we got there.'

'Did the horseman move?'

Docking stared. 'Just sat there looking at him, he says.'

Banham laughed sharply. 'It must have been Old Shanks. He's the regular headless horseman in these parts.'

Gently gave his glass another nudge. 'I think what Cator saw was a rainbow-shadow,' he said. 'Meaning there really was a horseman there. Watching Cator. Watching the body.'

'Is that . . . possible?' Banham gaped.

'Quite possible,' Gently said. He pushed the glass aside and rose. 'We're dealing with an interesting fellow,' he said.

Bayfield and his team received their briefing: Banham departed to H.Q. The locals had booked Gently in at the Royal William, and he took Docking there to lunch with him. In a cool room they ate a crab salad, made with fresh crabs from along the coast. While they ate Gently leafed through the file. Docking, a cautious man, offered no conversation.

Then they collected the Lotus from the yard, and Docking guided Gently to the High Hale road. Deserted and narrow, it led through a gentle country of russet fields and dark trees. Gently cruised the Lotus modestly, feeling his way into the silent landscape. Ahead, almost imperceptibly, the sweep of country was beginning to elevate.

They passed through a grove of thick-growing oaks, a sudden gloom after the brilliant light, then bracken and gorse began to replace standing crops on their left. The road was still rising. It ran straight for half a mile between tangled hedges, came to a point where it twisted downwards into a bracken-sided ravine.

'Left, here, sir,' Docking said quickly.

Left was a gap in the thick hedge. The Lotus bumped and pitched through it, wheels hopping on the ridged, iron-hard ground. Then suddenly they were out into an incandescent blueness, slanting dramatically to its own horizon: a fire-like, simmering blueness, bathing the eyes in its regal colour.

'Do we keep going?' Gently asked.

'Take the track to the right, sir,' Docking said.

Gently eased the Lotus into a stony path that carved deeply into the heather-bush. Slowly climbing, they bumbled along through smouldering plains of deep azure, stippled here and there with the hard gold and green patching of gorse.

'Now you'll see the village, sir.'

On their right the ground fell away precipitously. In a few more yards they reached a huge cleft, dropping dizzily to trees beneath. Gently parked. The cleft served as a frame for a majestic prospect of the coast: chequered fields, a clustering village, and the high-horizoned sea beyond. East of the village the land ran off in cliffs, backed by barrows and woody ridges; westward it sank into shingle banks and a tongue of salt marsh. The village was tree-sheltered, had its back to the sea, showed a flint tower and a white-sailed windmill. A tiny ship was moving below the horizon. A tractor tickered faintly in a field at their feet.

'Strange,' Gently said. 'Strange country.'

'Yes, sir,' Docking said. 'A place on its own. Used to be a well-known village for smuggling. There's deep water up to the shore.'

Gently drove on. Steep, bracken-choked coombes guarded the approach from the sea and the village. Inland, the heath began to show ridges and a few dark thickets of gnarled thorn. At the summit of the rise the track came to an end in a dense covert of gorse, where, commanding a vast view along the coast westward, stood an O.S. triangulation pedestal.

They got out.

'Reckon this'll give you some idea, sir,' Docking said. 'That's Clayfield up the coast, where you can see that round-towered church. It's high heath mostly all the way along, just a strip of arable in between. The road comes along skirting the salt marshes. That bit of shine in the distance is Bodney Creek.'

Gently shaded his eyes. 'This heath runs through to Clayfield?'

'Apart from the strip I mentioned, sir.'

'It wouldn't stop a horseman coming this way?'

'No, sir. Just a couple of field gates.'

Gently grunted. 'But if Mrs Rising was teaching children, she couldn't have been up here meeting Berney.'

'We only have her word so far,' Docking said. 'The same goes for Mr Rising, sir.'

They left the pedestal, Docking leading, and struck into the heath where the heather was thinnest. It was sweaty work. The spiteful sun bounced back at them from the rashes of stones and grey, packed sand. Quarter of a mile on they came to a valley. It sloped down narrowly between steep, brackeny banks. The bottom was lined with heather-bush through which ran a grudging, uncertain foot-track.

'This is the spot, sir.'

Docking pointed ahead to a hawthorn thicket on the left-hand slope. Ragged and gloomy, it offered a scant shade, its boughs reaching a little over the floor of the valley.

'Somewhere to wait . . .'

Docking mopped and nodded. 'That's the way I saw it, sir. If you're going to meet someone on the heath, it's as good a place as another.'

They reached the thicket. Around, below it, the churned heather-bush looked stale and wilted. Thin, straw-like grass where the body had lain had begun to resurrect itself.

Gently peered at the place, his eyebrows lifting.

'So . . . what did happen here?' he asked.

'How do you mean, sir?' Docking queried.

'Berney was killed on the spot where he met her.'

'That's how it looks, sir.'

'That's just how it looks.'

For a moment, Docking's expression was blank. Then his eyes widened.

'My God . . . she may still have been around!' he said.

Gently shrugged, looking about him, at the bracken banks, the thread of track. The valley continued sloping downwards, broadening, was closed at last by a distant ridge.

Suddenly, Gently went still.

'Look.'

On the far ridge, a horseman sat watching them.

He was visible for perhaps two seconds; then he vanished on the other side of the ridge.

CHAPTER THREE

'THE CHEEKY BASTARD!'

Docking, flushing up, took a couple of instinctive steps down the valley. But pursuit was pointless: he came to a stand, hands clenched, eyes glowering at the empty ridge.

Gently chuckled. 'No good,' he said. 'This is country where horsemen hold the cards.'

'But the nerve of it, sir!' Docking exclaimed. 'He wasn't giving a damn if we did see him.'

'Could you recognize him?'

'Well – no, sir. But we might have had some glasses.'

'And he might just be some innocent horse-rider, coming this way out of curiosity.'

Docking snorted. 'He cleared off pretty sharply. He knew we weren't just a couple of bird-watchers.' He turned eagerly. 'And another thing, sir. He was riding a dark-coloured horse.'

Gently nodded. 'And he was wearing dark clothes . . . and he struck me as sitting tall in the saddle.'

'Rising's a tall man, sir.'

'It proves nothing.'

'But sir, if we sent a Panda car round . . .'

Gently grinned at the local man. 'All right!' he said. 'Go back to the car and lay on a Panda. But observation only, understand? I don't want Rising put on his guard before I talk to him.'

Docking cantered away gratefully, his feet thumping on the hard ground. Gently shrugged and continued his inspection of the spot.

It was very quiet after Docking had gone. No bird or insect stirred in the valley. Up by the pedestal there had been a draught from the sea, but nothing of it reached down here. Airless, silent . . . much as it must have been on the afternoon of Tuesday, when Berney had come down the overgrown track to wait here, in the hot shade.

And the woman . . . she'd come up the valley? Gently shaded his eyes and stared down towards the ridge. Where had she come from, across the baking heath, two or three miles, to be approaching that way? Had she also been mounted? The conclusion seemed irresistible. Footing it, she'd have arrived there fagged out and in a mess. A horse-woman . . . like Mrs Rising. Living in that direction . . . like Mrs Rising. Who else could Berney have seen come over the ridge, ride up the valley?

So they'd met, and she'd tethered the horse – a stout hawthorn limb was handy – and they'd dallied in the shade, in the skimpy little bower with its sick grass. Had they seen the second rider coming, giving her time to mount and make her escape – or had he approached more circumspectly, appearing, say, on the ridge-top opposite?

Flicking sweat from his forehead, Gently began to scramble up the rough bracken-slope. Up there, anyway, would have been the horseman who'd thrown a scare into Cator. The slope was steep and the bracken tangled, but it was perhaps no obstacle to a well-managed horse: there were tumps and stony ridges to give support to probing hooves. He struggled over the top. Now, directly below him, lay the shaded nook and trampled heather. For a spy, mounted or unmounted, this was the perfect situation. But it told him nothing. All around him was iron ground and heather-bush, where a man or a horse could go and leave no trace of passage behind. This way, that way, the ridging heath stretched emptily to its skylines.

He stared grumpily for a while, then set off back to the car. Docking came to meet him.

'It's all set, sir,' he said. 'We've got a man watching Rising's place.'

'Fine,' Gently said. 'Tell me something – where did you find Berney's car?'

'Berney's car, sir? It was down below, near where we came in.'

'Why wasn't it up here?'

Docking stared blankly. 'Don't quite know, sir,' he said. 'There's good cover down there. He may have thought it was the safest place.'

'There's cover up here,' Gently said. 'And it's a lot nearer to where he was heading.'

'He needn't have come this way at all, sir,' Docking said. 'He could have cut across to the valley.'

'But still – it's farther?'

Docking nodded reluctantly.

'And it was a hot day,' Gently shrugged. 'Maybe Berney needed the exercise. After the hours he'd spent sitting around.'

They got in the car. Gently backed and turned it, set it bumping slowly down the track.

'It's still bothering me,' he said. 'I can't quite picture what happened out there.'

'Perhaps Rising can help us, sir,' Docking said meaningfully. 'By the time we get to Clayfield he should be back.'

'Only,' Gently said, 'we're not going to Clayfield. I want to talk to the widow.'

Docking said nothing.

High Hale was a dullish, huddling village that crowded too close to the crooked coast road. It ignored the sea: the land sloped up between, and nesting trees made a further barrier. What the houses of brick or flint pebbles looked out on was the stark reef of the lofted heath. Across the fields, above foot-slope trees, it spread darkly along the sky.

Berney's house, the Lodge, stood behind and above the village. A discreet Victorian residence, in greyed yellow brick, it was reached by a drive flanked with rhododendrons. A green Vitesse was parked at the door. Gently coasted the Lotus in behind it. As he and Docking got out, the door above opened and a girl dressed in slacks came down the steps.

'The police – again?'

She paused on the last step, her grey eyes taking them in boldly. She was twenty-one or -two, tallish, slender, with golden-blonde hair sweeping her shoulders. Her fine features were strikingly regular but they were pale and blurred under the eyes. She wore a loose open-necked shirt with the slacks. Her stomach was swollen and fruit-like.

'Mrs Berney,' Docking murmured.

Mrs Berney flicked her long hair. 'So what is this?' she said. 'Have you made an arrest – or am I in for another session of insinuation?'

'This is Chief Superintendent Gently,' Docking said hastily.

'Which means nothing to me,' Mrs Berney said.

'He's from London, ma'am. He's taking charge of the case.'

Mrs Berney eyed Gently. 'Wonderful,' she said.

Gently smiled and came forward. Mrs Berney kept eyeing him. Her expression was insolent, but her glance was keen. She gave another toss to her swirling hair, making the motion into an insult.

'Of course, I have heard of you,' she said.

'Thank you,' Gently said. 'And I'd heard of your brother.'

'Lachlan.' Her eyes held Gently's defiantly. 'He's great. A great poet. Truly great.'

'I'm hoping to meet him,' Gently said.

'He's the greatest poet writing today.'

'I don't know of a greater,' Gently said truthfully. 'I trust this business hasn't affected his work.'

She gave a small, bitter laugh. 'What do you want?'

'I have to talk to you. That's routine.'

She nodded. 'Of course. However inconvenient.'

'Is it inconvenient?'

'Oh, come in,' she said.

* * *

She led them into the house.

They passed through a broad staircase hall, carpeted and hung with framed maps, into a well-proportioned lounge lit by attractive bow windows. The effect was expensive. The floor was covered with an Indian carpet in pale, washed colours. The furniture, every piece matched, was meticulous Hepplewhite reproduction. The book-shelves were filled with polished bindings, a Tompion-style bracket clock stood on the mantelshelf, and the principal picture, in a heavily carved frame, was a lush landscape by Edward Seago.

'Sit if you want to.'

Mrs Berney rang a bell, then settled herself lightly on the sofa. Lithe, easy-moving in spite of her condition, she was much too young for that room.

'This will be your husband's taste . . .?'

She tipped her head. 'He probably furnished for his number one. Charlie was only a brewer, remember – draggy rooms made him feel comfortable.'

'You didn't mind?'

'It was Charlie's way. If I didn't like it I needn't have married him.'

'You loved him enough so it didn't matter.'

She swished her hair. 'Please. Stick to routine.'

A puffy-faced countrywoman answered the bell. Mrs Berney ordered iced beers. The woman glanced frowningly at the two policemen and gave a slight shrug as she went out. Docking, who'd stared at her, echoed the shrug, then wandered away to gaze through a window.

Gently seated himself in a Hepplewhite chair.

'Tell me about your husband,' he said.

32

Mrs Berney gave him a long, cool look. 'My husband loved me,' she said. 'That's the truth.'

'How did you meet him?'

She gestured. 'Charlie was a friend of the family,' she said. 'I think my father knew his father. He was always dropping in, over at the Manor. When I was a child he was Uncle Charlie, he used to play with Lachlan and me. Then I grew up.' She smoothed her long thigh. 'Marrying Charlie seemed the natural thing to do.'

'But it wasn't quite a . . . passionate affair?'

'I'm not sure what you mean.' She glanced down at her stomach. 'This took a little more than three months to happen, so presumably there was passion around somewhere.'

'He was twice your age.'

'Perhaps that's how I like it.'

'You'd know his reputation.'

'That's always a challenge.' She kept stroking her thigh. 'Anyway, he was passionate all right. It was me he wanted. I spoiled him for the others.'

Gently looked at her steadily. 'And you really believe that?'

She stared back at him. 'I know it's true. But don't let me upset your marvellous theories – my poor little pride will probably survive.'

The domestic returned with the beers, served in tall, stemmed glasses; Mrs Berney sipped hers sparingly, her eyes gazing past Gently. She wore no make-up, no jewellery, not even a ring on her finger. Her hair, simply long, flowed like fine spun-gold.

'So it was a happy marriage.'

'Entirely happy.'

'Losing your husband has been a great shock.'

She inclined her head. 'I'm a Stogumber,' she said. 'We don't get knocked off our base so easily.'

'But you loved him. And he loved you.'

'Perhaps you'd like me to break down,' she said. 'I'm twenty-one, I was married three months. It never had time to seem real in the first place.'

Gently shrugged and swallowed some beer.

'Let's talk about your husband's friends,' he said. 'On Monday he gave a party here. Who were the people he invited?'

She laughed. 'That's not very subtle. They were mostly friends of mine we invited – young couples, people I knew. Charlie arranged the party for me.'

'Are the Risings young people?'

'Jerry and Jill. They're old friends. Jill taught me to ride. We were over at Clayfield riding on Sunday, and naturally I asked them to come along.'

'But they were old friends of your husband's too?'

'Yes.' She gave a sling to her hair. 'Only don't waste your time digging scandal there – Charlie scarcely spoke to Jill all the evening.'

'Who did he speak to?'

'Leo, mostly. That's Leo Redmayne, father's cousin. And Lachlan. And Tommy Brightwell. But mostly he was just acting host.'

'Did you dance, play games?'

'We danced.'

'Your husband danced?'

'He danced with me.'

'That was discreet of him,' Gently said.

Mrs Berney gave him a hard stare. 'As a matter of fact,

34

he danced once with me, then he fell out and played the records for us. He certainly wasn't hanging round Jill Rising – or anyone else, if it comes to that.'

Gently nodded. 'So you noticed nothing.'

'Because there was nothing to notice,' she said.

'Not, of course, until after the guests had gone.'

Mrs Berney sat very straight, her eyes angry.

'So – you've been getting at Haynes,' she said. 'Oh, don't deny it! You see, I asked her. And I don't blame her for saying what she did – what else could she do, being hounded by you people? And it was true. She saw me grab something from Charlie. A sheet of paper – she said it was a letter. And that fitted your wonderful theory, didn't it? Of course, it was a letter Charlie'd had from a woman!' She breathed quickly. 'But you're wrong,' she said. 'Because, you see, it didn't happen to be a letter. And it belonged to me, not to Charlie. You're wrong all along the line.'

Gently shrugged. 'So what was it, Mrs Berney?'

'Why should I tell you what it was?'

'You don't have to,' Gently said. 'But if it is something innocent, you've no reason not to.'

'Something innocent!' She glared at him. 'All right, then, I will tell you. It was a poem Lachlan had brought to show me. Now admit you were wrong.'

'A poem . . . ?'

'Yes – a poem. Lachlan gave it to me as he was leaving. And I didn't want Charlie making fun of it, that's why I wouldn't let him have it.'

Gently stared. 'Do you have the poem?'

'Of course.'

35

'Do you mind if I see it?'

She hesitated. 'I'd sooner you didn't. And I'm quite certain Lachlan would sooner you didn't.'

'Why, Mrs Berney?'

'Because, because.' She gave the familiar flick of her hair. 'It's extremely personal. I always see Lachlan's poems, but this was written to be read by only one other person.'

'In fact, a love poem?'

'In fact, a love poem. And now you know all there is to know. I don't think Lachlan would ever have forgiven me if I'd let Charlie read it.'

Gently nodded. 'All the same, I think you should let me take a look at it.'

'And if I refuse?'

He made a gesture with his glass. 'You won't do that, will you, Mrs Berney?'

She glared a brief defiance at him, then rose sulkily and crossed to the Hepplewhite bureau. She returned with a folded sheet of notepaper which she dropped disdainfully into his hand. The poem was a sonnet. It was in typescript and bore no title and no signature. The type, unusually, was an italic, very clean and unworn. Gently read:

This aching empty all of me is crying
For absent You to fill it with your love,
And I am lost and my best part a-dying
To have you not this hollowness remove.

O world, why must that She, that only She,
Whose breast in my breast finds its proper mate,

Be to the loveless and indifferent free,
While I alone must stand aloof and wait?

We were not made for parting, she and I,
Though dragons guard the path our love must
    tread;
Man, Woman, we: our fate was in the sky,
And out of all the ages were we wed.

One of a hundred makes another's wife,
But You are me, and, parting, take my life.

Mrs Berney was watching him jealously.

'Now perhaps you do understand,' she said. 'Lachlan didn't mind me reading that, but it wasn't intended for Charlie's eyes.'

Gently shook his head. 'You say *your brother* wrote this?'

Her eyes sharpened. 'What do you mean?'

'Just that I've seen another example of his work – and this doesn't bear much resemblance to it.'

'But that's preposterous!' Her eyes snapped at him. 'Who else could possibly have written it?'

'There is another candidate,' Gently shrugged.

'Charlie?'

Gently said nothing.

Mrs Berney laughed scornfully. 'You'll never know what a joke that is,' she said. 'Lachlan's the only poet round here, the only one capable of writing like that. If Charlie had wanted to send someone a poem, he'd have got it from the *Golden Treasury*.'

'Did your husband have a typewriter?'

'Yes – and it doesn't have type like Lachlan's.'

'I'd like to see it, Mrs Berney.'

'Please do. Then you'll know for a fact that I'm not a liar.'

She jumped up. Gently followed her out of the room and along the hall. She threw open the door of a small, bleak study, furnished with a desk and a filing-cabinet. On the desk stood a typewriter. It was one of the smaller Olivettis. Mrs Berney took a sheet of paper from the desk drawer, threaded it into the typewriter, and hammered out a sentence with two fingers. She raised the sheet.

'Now are you happy?'

Gently stared at her, then pulled out the sheet. He laid it on the desk, side by side with the poem. The type was different – but the paper matched.

'Of course . . . a coincidence.'

'Not even that!'

She snatched open the drawer from which she'd taken the paper. The paper was protruding from a blue packet labelled: *Crampton (Stationers), The High, Low Hale*.

'Our only stationers, Superintendent. And the only typewriter bond they sell. If you live round here you use that – so your precious coincidence falls flat.'

Gently shrugged, still gazing at the poem.

'But it's all too ridiculous,' Mrs Berney nagged. 'If you won't believe me, ask Lachlan – it's as simple as that. He'll tell you.'

'I'm sure he will,' Gently said.

'And it'll be the truth!' Mrs Berney stormed. 'If you think he'd pretend it was his when it wasn't, you don't know poets, that's all.'

Gently tapped the poem. 'Perhaps more important! Who was the lady this was written to?'

She tossed her hair furiously. 'Ask him that too. Myself, I didn't have the nerve.'

'She's fairly obviously a married woman,' Gently said.

'That would scarcely worry a poet.'

'A woman not easy to gain access to.'

'So perhaps her husband keeps her locked up.'

Gently paused to study her: tall, defiant, her fine eyes blazing disdain, her pear-like stomach carried swaggeringly, as though the fact of motherhood was impersonal to her.

'This isn't a game, Mrs Berney,' he said. 'We're trying to find your husband's killer. We need your help – even if it means your acknowledging that your husband was unfaithful. You must know something. Why not tell us?'

She stared back at him, her eyes steady. 'No,' she said. 'I don't know. If it was as you think, I couldn't tell.'

'But you'd guess something?'

She shook her head. 'I'm probably too young and inexperienced. He wasn't sleeping with me much anyway – I wouldn't have it, with me like this.'

'Perhaps you weren't very close to him at all?'

The disdain sparked afresh. 'I was his goddess! Charlie was crazy, demented about me. If you don't understand that, you understand nothing.'

'But you weren't letting him sleep with you?'

'It didn't matter. He'd do anything I asked.'

'Wasn't that quite a big thing?'

She drew herself tall. 'Charlie loved me,' she said. 'He really loved me.'

CHAPTER FOUR

Gently kept the poem; Docking took down from Mrs Berney a list of the guests at the birthday party. Still angry-eyed, she watched them from the porch as they went down the steps to the Lotus. Gently tinkered the car down the drive and through the village to the coast road, then parked on a piece of bald verge. He handed the poem to Docking, and began filling his pipe.

Docking read the poem frowningly.

'I don't know about this, sir,' he said. 'But I reckon you brought out one point back there. She wasn't madly in love with Berney.'

Gently puffed smoke through his window. 'She didn't have to be,' he said. 'He was twice her age, an old friend of the family. A bit of affection was all it needed.'

'I reckon he was barmy, sir, marrying her.'

'It wouldn't be a quiet life,' Gently admitted.

'With a temper like that, sir. She'd ride him rotten. You can't wonder he was back to chasing other women.'

'So what about the poem?'

Docking did some more frowning. 'Well, anyway,

sir, it makes sense,' he said. 'And the bloke who wrote this was really skirt-struck. So perhaps that answers one or two of your questions.'

'You mean, about Berney's behaviour?'

'That's right, sir. He was standing on his head over this woman. She wasn't just a piece he was going to lay. He'd have jumped through hoops for this one.'

'She must be some woman,' Gently said.

Docking swayed his shoulders. 'That's a matter of taste, sir. Some men'll blow their top for a woman that you and me wouldn't see anything in.'

'Like Mrs Berney.'

'Yes, sir,' Docking nodded. 'She isn't one I'd want to have truck with. Of course, she's handsome, very handsome. But somehow . . . well, she leaves you cold.'

Gently puffed. 'Who do we have on the list?'

Docking took out his notebook and read the list through. Along with the Risings, Redmayne and Lachlan Stogumber it contained two married couples and four couples with names linked.

'I don't know all of them, sir,' Docking commented. 'But it looks the way she was telling us. There are a lot of youngsters, perhaps friends of hers. There's nobody here we know connects with Berney.'

'Any raving beauties?'

'Not to my knowledge, sir.'

'Horsemen?'

Docking shook his head. 'I'll have Bayfield check the list for us, sir. But just now all I know about is the Risings.'

As though he'd given it a cue, the R/T clicked and came through with a message from the Panda car at

Clayfield. Gerald Rising had been seen riding in from the heath, from the direction of High Hale. Gently acknowledged. He glanced at Docking.

'Let's get over there, sir,' Docking urged. 'Rising's the best prospect we've got, and this'll give us a handle with him.'

Gently puffed a couple of times, then started the engine and stirred the gears. Quite suddenly they were drifting along at seventy, with Docking gripping the grab-handle and staring hard ahead.

Clayfield consisted of a string of cottages separated from the road by a small green, and facing acres of salt marsh, beyond which low dunes hid the sea. A dreary village; it had no trees. The cottages looked weather-worn and unprosperous. A blackboard, nailed to the palings of one of them, offered fresh samphire for sale.

A single, narrow road led inland, and into this Docking directed Gently. The Lotus nosed upwards between steep banks shaggy with rank grasses, ragwort and scabious. Then the road levelled. On the left stretched heath, viewed between tangled thickets of bramble; on the right, among a few wind-bitten oaks, stood a red-brick house with a range of outbuildings.

'That's Rising's place, sir . . . another old rectory.'

Gently grunted and turned in at the gates. A short, rather weedy drive led them to a sweep at the front of the house. An extension of the drive passed to the left. Gently let the Lotus idle along it. It brought them to a stableyard and a railed paddock set out with a number of low jumps. A woman in riding drag stood in the paddock, giving instructions to some children mounted on ponies. As the Lotus halted, the first of the ponies began bumping energetically towards a jump.

'She'll be Mrs Rising . . . ?'

Docking nodded. She was too far off for them to see her features. The tailored drag showed a full figure and gave a firm line to her strong bust. As they watched, the pony rattled the jump, and her voice reached them, clear and pleasant. Then she moved a few, confident steps and signalled the next pony to the jump.

'You wanted to speak to me?'

Gently turned. A man had silently come up behind them. He was tall, in his middle forties, and wore breeches and an open-necked shirt. He had a seamed, tanned, square-boned face and short, wiry hair, going grey. His eyes were narrowed, as though he had spent a lot of time looking into the sun.

'Gerald Rising?'

'That's me.' He spoke with a hard, down-under accent.

'I'm Chief Superintendent Gently.'

Rising's thin lips curled. 'I'm expecting you. Marie just rang to say you were around.'

'Marie?'

'Mrs Berney.'

'That was considerate of her,' Gently said.

'Oh, we're considerate people round here,' Rising said. 'Step out and make yourselves at home.'

Gently and Docking got out of the Lotus. Rising stood watching them with his half-grin. In a battered way, he was a handsome man, with a boyish cast beneath his lines. He stood jauntily, thumbs hooked in pockets, body slanted back a little from the hips. His shirt was of navy-blue linen and his breeches a grey cavalry twill.

'So why were you expecting us?' Gently asked.

Rising nodded his head towards the stables. 'I'm the lad who owns the horses,' he said. 'Where else would any policeman start looking?'

'And that's the only reason?'

'About it.' Rising's eyes slitted a little. 'Unless you've come up with something new, something that isn't in the grapevine.'

'What would that be?' Gently said.

Rising shook his head, grinning. 'Play it square, sport,' he said. 'I'm not guessing up answers for you.'

Gently nodded, his stare blank. 'Where were you this afternoon?' he said.

'Exercising a horse,' Rising said. 'I've just come from rubbing him down.'

'Do you mind if we see him?'

'Should I mind?'

'It's up to you,' Gently shrugged.

Rising paused, then he unhooked his thumbs. 'This way, gentlemen,' he said.

He led them across the paved yard to a range of recently built stabling. Horses, hearing the clump of his boots, pushed their curious muzzles over the half-doors. Rising buzzed and made throat noises to them and gave them fondling pats as he passed. He stopped at a door near the end, over which was leaning a tall, munching chestnut.

'Meet Ned,' he said. 'Ned Kelly. Ned, these gents are a couple of policemen.'

The chestnut curled its lip and blew softly through its nostrils, then went on stolidly with its munching.

Gently patted the handsome muzzle. The chestnut eyed him with complaisant interest. He let his hand stray over its neck, his fingers burrow in the coarse mane.

'Oh, it's damp all right,' Rising said. 'Fresh sweat. Why should I kid you about the horse?'

'You tell me,' Gently said. 'What was he doing over at High Hale?'

'High Hale?' Rising's eyes puckered. 'Who says he was over at High Hale?'

'Wasn't he?'

'No, he darned well wasn't! I took him for a loosener to Clayfield Warren.'

Gently glanced at Docking, who nodded unwillingly. 'It's in the same direction, sir,' he said. 'Clayfield Warren's towards Hale, but up this end and going inland.'

'And that's where he went,' Rising said. 'Look, what the devil is this all about? If you think I've been up to something, why not ask me straight out?'

Gently gave him a flat stare. 'Never mind,' he said.

'Yes, but I do mind,' Rising said. 'I've been sitting on a bomb ever since Tuesday, just because I happen to run a stable. And it's all a load of old cobblers. You've been up a creek from the start. If Charlie was killed by a horse like you say, there's only one around here could have done it.'

Gently shrugged. 'You should know.'

'Not one of mine!' Rising snapped. 'If I had a horse with a crook temper I soon wouldn't have any customers.'

'And it was that sort of horse?'

'What else? No ordinary horse would attack a man.'

'Not if he was put to it?'

Rising feinted a spit. 'Can't you see that's where you've gone wrong?' he said. He came closer to Gently. 'Listen,' he said. 'There's a horse, a stallion, with a vicious temper. We've had him here on service a couple of times, and I wouldn't let a customer as much as see him. He's on the spot. He gets loose. He runs into Charlie along that gully. Charlie sees he's a stray and he makes to collar him – and whacko! That's Charlie's lot. Doesn't that make sense – a lot more sense than somebody having a go at Charlie?'

Gently hesitated. 'Which horse is this?'

'The one that's been under your nose all the time! That evil black bastard at the Home Farm. His stable's only a mile from where you found Charlie.'

'A *black* horse?'

'Right. A black. Bred a hunter, stands eighteen hands.'

'With a killer temper?'

'Right again. Nat Creke can handle him, but I wouldn't try.'

'Creke's the farmer, sir,' Docking put in. 'We have checked that horse sir, if you remember. It was in its stable all day Tuesday. Creke exercised it in the evening.'

Rising laughed. 'That's Nat's tale. Show me how you're going to prove it.'

'Can you disprove it, sir?' Docking said.

Rising slitted his eyes at him, laughed again.

Gently gave a few pats to Ned's munching muzzle. 'So we'll follow it up,' he said. 'It's a possible theory. And meantime you weren't at Low Hale this afternoon – just out of curiosity, to look at the spot?'

46

'No I wasn't,' Rising said. 'I was where I told you.'

'Then we'll get on to something else,' Gently said. 'Last Sunday Berney and his wife were here riding. Perhaps you can tell me something about that.'

Rising pulled back a little, his eyes probing, his heavy hands crooking at his sides.

'That's a queer sort of thing to ask me,' he said. 'What's last Sunday got to do with it?'

'That's what I want to know,' Gently said. 'The Berneys did come here riding, didn't they?'

'Suppose they did,' Rising said. 'Sunday's the day when everyone comes.'

'So tell me about it,' Gently said.

Rising shook his head, his hands working. 'It was just like any other Sunday,' he said. 'Charlie rang in the morning to book two horses. We were full up in the afternoon. Charlie'd booked for three p.m. Leo Redmayne and her brother were here. They all went riding down to the beach.'

'They went together?' Gently said.

'Near enough,' Rising said. 'Marie and her brother went off first, then Leo, then Charlie. Charlie's saddle was loose, he says, so he waited for me to tighten the straps for him. But the beach was where they were going. They'd decided that before they mounted.'

Gently nodded. 'What other riders went that way?'

Rising flipped his hand. 'I don't keep an eye on them. Jill took her pony-string down there, but mostly the customers stick to the heath.'

'Your wife went that way?'

'Yes. Maybe she can tell you.'

'She set out about the same time as the Berneys?'

'She let them go first to get them out of the way. The pony-string isn't a fast mover.'

'I see,' Gently said. 'So it went like this. First, Mrs Berney in company with her brother. Then Mr Redmayne. Then Mr Berney. Then your wife with the string of ponies.'

'Right,' Rising said. 'Is that supposed to add up to something?'

Gently shrugged. 'Would you say it did?'

Rising slitted his eyes for a moment, then hooked a thumb in his breeches pocket.

'Let's come to that party now,' Gently said. 'When did you get your invitation?'

'They spoke to Jill about it,' Rising said sulkily. 'I was out with a starter when they got back.'

'Didn't you want to go to it?'

'Right,' Rising said. 'There's plenty to do here without parties. Only Jill and Marie are great buddies, so it was fixed up over my head.'

'Jill and Marie,' Gently said. 'So you went to this party a bit reluctantly. But no doubt you cheered up when you got there – a few drinks, dancing, some amusing people?'

Rising aimed a kick at the stable wall. 'All right, it wasn't so brilliant. I've been to some other parties of Charlie's, and they had more steam than Monday's.'

'How wasn't it brilliant?'

'It didn't jell. Charlie and Marie didn't circulate. Marie was stuck with her brother and Leo. Charlie acted like he couldn't be bothered.'

'He stayed in the background.'

Rising nodded. 'That's what you want to hear, isn't it? And it's true enough, he just sat around. The party was dead on its feet by eleven.'

'Didn't he dance?'

'Yes. With his wife.'

'With nobody else?'

Rising hesitated. 'If he did, I didn't notice,' he said. 'I happened to be dancing with my wife, too.'

'Of course,' Gently said. 'And there were no incidents.'

Rising swung his foot, said nothing.

'Then . . . or later.'

Rising looked at him. A flush was showing in his creased cheeks.

'Now look,' Rising said. 'Me, I'm an Aussie, and I don't much like your bloody methods. Where I come from we talk straight, and if that won't do we try this.' He stropped the knuckles of one hand across the palm of the other. 'So what are you getting at, sport?' he said.

Gently laid a finger on Rising's fist. 'This won't help you,' he said. 'Drop it.'

Rising's eyes thinned. 'You think I wouldn't,' he said.

'I think you wouldn't,' Gently said.

Rising snatched his fist away suddenly. 'You bastard,' he said. 'You're on about Jill and Charlie, aren't you? That's how your stinking policeman's mind works – Jill and Charlie, and me for patsy.'

'That's how my mind works,' Gently shrugged.

'Yeah, that's how it works,' Rising said. 'And you'd better make it work some other way, sport, because there's no percentage in that.'

49

'The gossip isn't true?'

'What gossip?' Rising snarled.

'Gossip we've been hearing,' Gently said smoothly.

'There hasn't been any gossip!'

Gently shook his head, stared mildly at Rising's furious glare.

'Look,' Rising said, moving closer, 'it's a bloody try-on, and you know it. Charlie's been pals with us for years and never a whisper about him and Jill. There wouldn't be. She isn't that sort of woman. She couldn't do it and me not know. And if any creeping bastard had said so I'd have beat him into a pulp.'

'The way we found Berney,' Gently said.

Rising's eyes thinned to points. 'Oh no,' he said. 'It won't do, sport. You're never going to hang that one on me. I was right here all day Tuesday.'

'Can you prove it?'

'Can you disprove it?' Rising sent a leer at Docking. 'I say I was here, and I was here. Look, you can see what I was doing.'

He turned abruptly and marched across to a building which had probably been the old coach-house. Gently and Docking followed. Rising pushed open the door, stood aside to let them enter.

'There. Run your eye over them.'

The interior had been converted into a workshop. Along one side ran a carpenter's bench with racks of tools mounted behind it. A miniature circular saw stood under the window and a stack of new timber lay by the wall. In the centre of the floor stood four freshly painted jumps, with splashings of paint lying around them.

'That's what I was doing Tuesday – finishing off these

new jumps. And Jill, she was out with the kids – and she didn't take them to High Hale.'

'You were here alone . . . ?'

'When Jill wasn't here. Our domestic only comes mornings.'

'So she's your alibi, you're hers.'

'Try to beat it,' Rising said. 'Try to beat it.'

Gently moved to one of the jumps and ran his fingers over the moistly silky fresh paint. 'I may do just that,' he said. 'Who were the kids who went with your wife?'

'You leave the kids out of it,' Rising said. 'I wouldn't know who they were anyway.'

'But your wife will know?'

'And leave her out of it! I'm not having Jill upset with dirty scandal.'

A shadow fell in the doorway: they turned to look. The woman in riding drag was standing there.

'And what scandal can that be?' she asked coolly.

'Jill!' Rising said. 'You get out of here.'

Jill Rising didn't get out. She stood looking at the policemen with a determined expression on her handsome face. She was younger than her husband, perhaps in her mid-thirties, and she had firm brown eyes and dark hair worn short. Her figure was majestic. A voluptuous bust rounded out pushingly beneath the black jacket, and the fine spring of hip and calf were not concealed by her jodhpurs.

'What scandal?' she repeated. 'I can't think of any that would upset me.'

'Jill,' Rising said appealingly. 'Just do what I say, Jill. I can handle what's going on here.'

Jill Rising laughed. 'I doubt it,' she said. 'The tone of your voice didn't sound reassuring. And if there's scandal being talked which I shouldn't hear, then of course it has to do with me and Charlie.'

'Look, Jill, will you leave it?' Rising implored.

'Don't be absurd, Jerry,' Jill Rising said. 'If these gentlemen have been listening to gossip, they'll certainly want to ask me if there's any truth in it.'

'It's filthy lies!'

'Is it?' she said.

'Oh my God, you know it is.'

'I know nothing of the sort,' Jill Rising said. 'Charlie made passes at me from the start.'

Rising pulled back from her. 'That's a lie!'

'Oh, relax, Jerry,' Jill Rising said. 'Charlie couldn't help it. He was made that way. With him it was like a nervous twitch.'

'But you never told me,' Rising snapped.

'Because you're too impetuous,' Jill Rising said. 'You'd have knocked him about, then there'd have been a lawsuit, and all about nothing except Charlie's being Charlie. *I* didn't mind. I rather liked it. I'd have felt hurt if he'd made me an exception.'

'But . . . holy Josephine!' Rising said.

'Isn't that what the policemen want to know?'

'You can bet it is!'

'So,' Jill Rising said. 'Now they know it – for what it's worth.'

She turned calmly to Gently. Gently cleared his throat. 'And . . . this . . . had been going on for some time?'

'Ever since Charlie began coming here,' Jill Rising said. 'Even before we'd been introduced.'

'The slimy Casanova!' Rising burst out.

'Did he make a pass at you on Sunday?'

Jill Rising shook her head. 'Not since he married Marie. Charlie had reformed. He really loved her, you know.'

'He made no approach to you?'

'Not of that kind. I rode part of the way to the beach with him. He seemed a bit absent-minded, not quite his old self. I thought perhaps he'd had a tiff with Marie.'

Gently nodded. 'Did you speak to her?'

'Yes. We all met up on the beach.'

'Was she her old self?'

'Oh yes, Marie. It takes a good deal to throw her.'

'But I'd have thrown *him*,' Rising growled in his throat. 'Hell, when I think about that party . . .'

'He means parading me there,' Jill Rising said quickly. 'In a plunge-neck dress, for Charlie to ogle. But really, it wasn't a very bright party. Charlie was dull as an old bear. If you think he had a woman on his mind you could be right, but it wasn't anybody at the party.'

Gently hesitated. 'Is that what you thought?'

Jill Rising smiled brightly. 'It crossed my mind. It couldn't have been money, because Charlie was rolling, and with Charlie there was practically only one other thing.'

'And you had a guess,' Gently said. 'Knowing Berney so well?'

'Perhaps,' Jill Rising said. 'But I'd nothing to go on. As I told you, Charlie'd reformed after he married Marie. He'd broken off with all his old playmates.' She looked at Gently squarely, her brown eyes forceful. 'I'm your best bet,' she said, 'only it wasn't me. Charlie knew

53

he had nothing coming from me. Over the years, the message had got through.'

Gently paused, still holding her eyes. 'But he'd tried,' he said, 'over the years?'

'I've admitted that. He made passes.'

'Including writing you poems . . . like this?'

He pulled out the poem and shoved it at Jill Rising. She flushed suddenly and put her hand out with reluctance. Gerald Rising stepped closer to her. His mouth was pressed tight. Jill Rising fumbled with the sheet, got it open, began reading. Then she laughed a little breathlessly.

'Charlie never wrote this!'

'Here, let me look,' Gerald Rising said. He took hold of the sheet, his eyes puckering, and read the poem right through.

'You agree?' Gently said.

Rising nodded. 'We've only got one poet round here, sport.'

'It's one of Lachlan's,' Jill Rising laughed. 'And it wasn't written to me, I assure you.'

'You've never seen it before?'

'I . . . never!'

'For example, on Monday.'

She shook her head, her face hot.

'You?' Gently said to Rising.

'Me neither,' Rising said. 'If you want to know about this you'd better ask Marie's brother.'

Gently took the poem and stowed it away again. The two Risings stood silent, their eyes turned from him. Jill Rising's starch had gone out of her. Gerald Rising's thumbs had crept back into his pockets.

'That leaves me with one question,' Gently said. 'I'd like the names of the children who accompanied Mrs Rising on Tuesday.'

'I can give them to you,' she said in a low voice. 'But it may not help much. I picked them up after school.'

'After school,' Gently said. 'When was that?'

'It was quarter to four,' Jill Rising said.

'I see,' Gently said. 'Still, I'll have the names.'

Gerald Rising's thumbs hooked tighter.

CHAPTER FIVE

T HE LOTUS WAS hot. Gently switched on the fan as
they turned out of the stable yard. From Rising's
drive one could see the sea, but there was little breeze
coming from that direction. A black thunder-fly was
trapped behind the windscreen and Docking squashed it
with a well-aimed prod. They tinkered through the
gates into the narrow road and coasted down to the
silent village.

'Amusing people,' Gently said.

Docking trailed his fingers in the moving air. 'One
thing's certain, sir,' he said comfortably. 'They don't
have an alibi worth a wet fag.'

Gently gave his slow nod. 'What did you think of the
lady?'

Docking watched the road for some moments before
replying. 'I think she was doing a nice job, sir,' he said
at last. 'Until you gave her a jolt with that poem. Now
I think she was just trying to beat us to the punch. I
reckon Berney did more than make a pass at her. And I
reckon Rising knew about it, too, for all the front he
tried to put up.'

'You think it blew up at the party?'

'Maybe afterwards, sir. There was something hap-pened about that poem. Perhaps Rising saw Berney slip it to her, and somehow she got it back to Berney.'

'Then Mrs Berney took it from him.'

'That'd be how it was, sir. And Mrs Berney isn't going to let on because then she'd be giving herself a motive.'

Gently eased for the junction with the coast road. 'There's another angle to it,' he said. 'I'm not so sure that Rising's reactions were faked – not about the poem, in any case.'

'How do you mean, sir?'

Gently smoothed a gear-change. 'Lachlan Stogumber was also at the party.'

Docking stared at the road. 'You think he did write the poem?'

'It's what everyone's telling us,' Gently shrugged. He paused to let the Lotus skim up to sixty. 'Let's look at it that way a moment,' he said. It's Lachlan Stogumber who's Mrs Rising's lover, who tried to slip her the poem at the party. Mrs Rising doesn't get it, or if she gets it she decides it's too dangerous to hang on to. So she slips it to her friend Marie, who is careless enough to let Berney get hold of it.'

'I'm still not with you, sir,' Docking said.

Gently stroked the wheel. 'What would Berney do? He's always had a fancy for Mrs Rising, and now he's in a position to use blackmail.'

Docking sat up straight. 'By crikey, sir!'

'But where does that get us?' Gently said.

'He'd send a message to her, sir – perhaps risk ringing

57

her – and make her come out to meet him on the heath.' Gently hunched a shoulder. 'And when she got there?'

Docking's eyes were large. 'It didn't need a man, sir. Just a rider on a horse with a big enough motive – and that's what she was when she met Berney.'

Gently chuckled. 'It still leaves some loose ends – like Berney's odd behaviour on Tuesday.'

'But it fits the rest, sir,' Docking said eagerly. 'Including the point you just made about Rising and the poem. Of course, he'd never seen the poem. She just glanced at it, but he read it. And the way she behaved, sir, I think he was catching on. If he didn't know before, he knows now.'

'There's still Berney's behaviour to explain.'

'He could've been scared stiff of Rising, sir.'

'And our rider on his dark horse.'

'Perhaps that fellow doesn't come into it.'

Gently laughed at Docking's fervent expression. 'There's one more objection. Would Mrs Rising have done it?'

'We can show opportunity, sir. And a pretty fat motive.'

'But would she have done it?'

Docking was silent.

The Lotus slid docilely into High Hale, where the clock on the flint church tower was showing four thirty. Above the trees above the cottages the bland front of The Lodge displayed its slatted windows. Gently eased to walking-pace.

'It's an amusing theory,' he said. 'But just now we'll keep it on the file. Meanwhile there's that stallion

58

Rising was good enough to mention – I think we should take a look at that.'

'That's at Home Farm,' Docking said glumly. 'It's at the back of the heath, off the Low Hale road.'

'And the Manor House,' Gently said. 'Where would that be?'

'It's in the same direction,' Docking said. 'Sir.'

They drove up past the heath again and as far as the grove of oaks. Here one of the narrow roads to which Gently was becoming accustomed bore away to the right. It skirted the heath on one hand and standing crops on the other, separated from them by low banks where grasses tangled with stubs of hawthorn. Then a plastered farmhouse appeared to the left, half-concealed by the lift of the fields. It had steep roofs of glazed blue pantiles and was hemmed by brick outbuildings and bushy elders.

'Does Creke have any neighbours?' Gently asked.

'No, sir,' Docking said. 'Farmers don't go in for them.'

'How far is the Manor House from here?'

Docking considered. 'I'd say another mile, sir.'

They reached a junction with a concrete track which led across the fields to the farmhouse. The junction was marked by an island of trees in which nestled a farm building and a pond scummed with weed. In the field opposite a big combine-harvester was puffing steadily through a stand of barley, while under the hedge lay four or five bicycles. A man lounged by them, smoking, watching.

'Farmer Creke, sir.'

Gently parked the Lotus. Creke made no motion to come across. A lean, hard-framed man with greasy black hair, he leaned against a field-gate, his eyes inspecting them. He was around fifty, probably six foot, and his black hair extended to ghostly sideboards. He was smoking a small, sooty briar from which smoke rose in regular puffs.

Gently got out and walked over to him.

'Mr Creke?'

Creke looked him over with quick grey eyes. He shifted his pipe to the side of his mouth. 'That's me,' he said. 'Who are you?'

Gently introduced himself. Creke nodded. He nostrilled a couple of wisps of smoke.

'So what's on now?' he said. 'Your blokes were here Wednesday. I can't tell you more now than I could then.'

'Do you know Gerald Rising?' Gently asked.

Creke took a few draws. 'What about him?'

'We've been talking to him.' Gently said. 'About your black stallion. About the way you can handle it when it's out on service.'

Creke spat past his pipe. 'He's a big-mouth,' he said. 'I'll have a word with him too when I see him.'

'But he's right about the horse?'

'Right nothing,' Creke said. 'Prince is quiet as a baby if you don't rattle him.'

'But if you do . . . ?'

Creke eased himself off the gate. 'Let me give you a tip,' he said. 'Rising's an Aussie. He didn't know the first blind thing about horses when he came up this way a few years back. His missus taught him all he knows and

60

that'd go on a picture postcard. He doesn't know a horse and he can't ride one. What he says about them is squit.'

'So,' Gently said. 'The stallion's a quiet horse.'

'He's quiet as a dozen others I know.'

'You'd let your child ride him?'

Creke wagged his head. 'He's eighteen hands,' he said. 'He's a bloody horse!'

As he spoke a deep clear neigh sounded from the building amongst the trees.

'That's him,' Creke said. 'He could hear my voice. If you want to see a horse, come and look at him.'

The building stood well back in the trees with the weed pond lying in front of it. Great, double doors were yawning open to reveal a shadowy, unlit interior. Creke marched them in. They were met by stable-smell and the sound of ponderously moving hooves. From a loosebox in the corner protruded the serpent-like head of a huge, jet-black horse.

'Prince boy, Prince, Prince.'

Creke strutted up to the massive animal. At once it arched its glinting neck and began to fuss his face with its lips. It snorted and made low whinnying noises. Creke buzzed and patted and ruffled its forelock. Then he gave it a firm slap on the neck, when it snatched its head up with a chuckling neigh.

'There,' Creke said. 'There. Would either of you gents like to shake hands with him?'

Gently shrugged and glanced at Docking, who shook his head very firmly.

'Ah, you're no horsemen,' Creke said, grinning. 'It's a privilege to meet a horse like Prince. Look at his shine. Look at his eye. There isn't a better sire in England.'

The horse chuckled again, its head held proudly, its smoky eyes staring down at them. Then it made a little dart in Gently's direction, its lips curling from great yellow teeth.

'Wheesh, Prince boy!' Creke said, patting him.

'Where does this horse come from?' Gently asked.

'He comes out of Leicestershire,' Creke said. 'My brother put me on to him. He farms out that way.'

'A hunter, was he?'

'That's right. He used to hunt with the Quorndon.'

'But they decided to sell him.'

Creke nodded.

Gently paused. 'Why?' he asked.

Creke leaned back against the rails of the loosebox, his hand toying with the great beast's mouth.

'I could tell you a lie,' he said. 'But I won't. They had some trouble with him over there.'

'Go on,' Gently said. 'What trouble?'

'I reckon someone treated him wrong,' Creke said. 'He's a proud bugger, he won't have it. He laid into a stable-boy in his box.'

'He killed him?'

Creke shook his head. 'Otherwise he wouldn't be here today. But he duffed up the bloke enough so's the owner thought it was smart to get rid of him. That's the tale, and I don't mind telling it. He's never been any trouble with me. He's a stallion mind you, he needs handling – but that's all. He's no problem.'

'A stranger could ride him,' Gently said.

'That's right,' Creke said. 'If I told Prince he could.'

'And a stranger could catch him.'

Creke's quick eye flickered. 'Would this be one of Rising's notions?' he asked.

Gently hesitated, then nodded.

'I guessed it would be,' Creke said. 'Next time I'm over at Clayfield I'll turn Prince loose and see if Mr. Jerry Rising can catch him.' He gave the horse's cheek a ruffle. 'Not Berney nor no one could catch him,' he said. 'Once he was off on his own on that heath, I'd be the only one who'd get near him.'

'And, of course, he never is on his own on the heath?'

'Do you think I'm stupid?' Creke said.

Gently motioned to the two strong bolts that secured the gate of the loosebox. 'People do make mistakes,' he said.

Creke checked a moment, staring at the bolts, but then gave a decided shake of his head. 'There's only me sees after this horse,' he said. 'And I never make mistakes like that.'

'He was here Tuesday evening?'

'He was here. I came down about seven to give him his run. And the gate was shut then, and the bolts shot, the way I'd left them in the morning.'

Gently nodded. 'Where did you exercise him?'

'Up round the farm,' Creke said.

'Not on the heath?'

'Why should I?' Creke said. 'It's the farm I want to keep my eye on.'

'Then you wouldn't have had him out there this afternoon?'

Creke stared from under his dark brows. 'Would that be likely?' he said. 'In the middle of harvest, with a fine spell due to break any time? We've been up on the fifteen-acre all day, and just now got a start on the barley. The only time I have for Prince is in the evening – and not always then, this time of year.'

The big horse whinnied, as though in confirmation.

'And that's how it was on Tuesday?' Gently said.

'Just like that,' Creke said. 'We were over on the glebe land. Ask some of the chaps, they'll soon tell you.'

Gently was silent. His eyes glanced round the building, at the corn-bins, hay-rack, the shelf of brushes; at the fine black saddle that hung from a peg, with matching reins and bridle beside it. His glance came back to Creke, who was watching him closely.

'So now you know about everything,' Creke said. 'It wasn't old Prince who did that job Tuesday.'

Gently's stare was expressionless. 'Let's step outside,' he said.

They left the great stallion snuffling and tramping and went out into the sunlight. The pond stretched peacefully before the building and the trees clustered thickly behind and above it. From the field across the track came the sound of the combine, but it was distant and muffled by a line of hedge. The track slanted away between hedges and crops and vanished at last behind the trees.

'A quiet spot . . .'

Gently picked up a stone and tossed it in the water to ripple the pond-weed.

'And a handy spot.'

He picked up another stone and tossed it over the hedge, where it rattled on the road. He turned to Creke.

'Quiet and handy – and invisible from the house. And nobody here from morning till night. Just the horse . . . and his saddle.'

Creke's black brows hooked up 'Now, listen—' he began.

'Do you walk down here from the house?' Gently said.

'I've got a bike, but—'

'You don't bother to get a car out?'

Creke stood staring, his mouth open.

Gently pointed to a space beside the building. 'Someone's parked a car there lately,' he said. 'Out of the sun. Out of sight. Where you wouldn't see it from the track.'

'But that was my car—'

'What's the make?'

'Morris. A Morris Oxford Traveller.'

Gently gave the confused markings an appraising look. 'This was something smaller,' he said. 'Perhaps an 1100.'

'But I'm telling you it was mine!' Creke exclaimed. 'Last night I fetched a sack of oats down here.'

'And you parked over there,' Gently said. 'Not beside the doors?'

'That's right,' Creke said. 'That's just what I did.'

Gently shook his head. 'In my book,' he said, 'someone parked his car there who didn't want it seen. And there's only one reason to park in this spot.' He jerked his head towards the doors.

Creke's sharp eyes bored at Gently, and for a moment his knuckles were white. Then the eyes flickered, and he loosened. He gave an ingratiating little chuckle.

'All right – you've got me! Someone could have parked there, and I should never be the wiser. But I reckon it was more likely a couple of lovers than a person interested in the horse. That cock won't fight.'

'Why?' Gently said.

'Isn't that obvious?' Creke said. 'If a stranger went in there interfering with Prince, he'd likely finish up the same way as the stable-boy.'

'Who's talking about a stranger?' Gently said.

Creke's eyes jumped at him. 'Aren't we?' he said.

'I'm not,' Gently said. 'I'm talking about someone who knows that horse, who can ride him.'

Creke looked at him; looked away. 'I reckon you know more than I do,' he said. 'There's maybe chaps over at Melton who can ride him, but they aren't around here.'

'Someone much closer,' Gently said.

'Nobody I know,' Creke said.

'From the village,' Gently said.

Creke shook his head.

'From the Manor.'

'No,' Creke said. 'No. There's nobody.'

'Not Gerald Rising.'

Creke's laugh was genuine. 'I'd like to see that Aussie try!'

'Mrs Rising.'

Creke hesitated. 'I'm not saying *she* couldn't. But she bloody doesn't.'

'So,' Gently said. 'That just leaves you. He's a one-man horse, and you're his master. He was safe in his box all Tuesday, and you were up on the glebe land along with your men.'

Creke stiffened slightly. 'That's it,' he said. 'And it's the truth. You'll never make it different.'

'I wonder,' Gently shrugged. 'Was Berney a friend of yours?'

'Maybe he was,' Creke said. 'Maybe.'

'And a friend of your wife's?'

'You'd better ask her,' Creke said. His mouth twisted. 'She's up at the house.'

'Sir,' Docking said quickly. 'We've spoken to Mrs Creke. I understand she has some disability.'

'In fact, she's a bloody cripple,' Creke said. He spat in the pond. 'But you go and see her.'

CHAPTER SIX

T HERE WAS NOTHING more to be got out of Creke –
certainly nothing more he proposed to tell them.
He stuck his pipe in his mouth, leered, and strutted away
to join the workers. Not a man you'd easily over-reach
. . . Gently watched him till he'd disappeared through
the field-gate: a hard, obstinate, confident figure, a man
used to wrestling with lands and seasons.

'Do you reckon he was lying, sir?' Docking said, also
watching.

Gently grunted. 'One thing's certain. If anybody rides
this horse besides Creke, the odds are that Creke knows
who.'

'You don't think it might have strayed, sir?'

Gently shook his head. 'That theory was never on. If
Berney went on the heath for a clandestine meeting, he
wouldn't advertise it by returning stray horses. No, if
this was the horse, then it had a rider – and the rider is
someone known to Creke. He may not have known the
horse was out, but even that . . .' Gently shrugged. 'Let's
take another look at him.'

They went back into the building. The black stallion

hadn't shifted from its post by the gate. It stood quite
still, ears alert, its prominent eyes staring fixedly. A huge
presence of a horse: it had the power of making them
feel intruders. It showed no fear, no uneasiness – here
were men: lesser creatures.

'Do you ride?' Gently asked Docking.

'No, sir – at least, I haven't ridden since I was a
nipper.'

'If he was a strange horse, would you tackle him?'

'Not unless I was tired of life, sir,' Docking said.

'I think he's our horse,' Gently said.

He walked up to the gate, to the stallion. It sent loud
warning breaths through its nostrils, but didn't budge or
twitch a muscle.

'I'd come away if I were you, sir,' Docking said. 'I
fancy Rising wasn't so far out.'

The stallion breathed faster and showed its teeth; its
ears flattened along its skull. Then it dropped its head
quickly with a shrill neigh. Gently lunged backwards.
Teeth clashed on air.

'God – the black devil!' Docking burst out.

'He's our horse,' Gently said.

'If he is I'm getting a destruction order,' Docking
said. 'The black bastard. He should be in a zoo.'

The stallion backed off, its hooves scraping, and came
to a stand in the centre of the box. There it raised its
head high and gave a clamorous neigh.

Gently watched it musingly. 'But it's a horse,' he said.

They got back in the Lotus and continued driving along
the narrow road. Soon the fields on the left gave way to
trees, a deep plantation of beech and conifers. Then

these thinned. An amphitheatre appeared, edged with copper beeches, elms and chestnuts; and here, perfectly sited, lay a long, low, Elizabethan house. It was built of the local rust-red brick and presented a front of irregular small gables. Shallow wings flanked either end and there were three clusters of ornamental brick chimneys.

'We're rather proud of this place, sir,' Docking said. 'It's been here since 1584.'

'What about the Stogumbers?' Gently said. 'Are they an old family?'

'Probably been here as long, sir,' Docking said. 'Once they used to be important people, but I reckon death duties took care of that. They still own some land around here.'

'Including the Home Farm?'

'Yes, sir – including that.'

Gently turned off between tall stone pillars, each topped with a stone gryphon, and drove between hedges of clipped yew to the gravel strip that fronted the house. Here there was a circular flowerbed where an elderly man knelt weeding. He looked up as the Lotus arrived, then got stiffly to his feet. Gently parked and got out. The man came over.

'I'm looking for Mr Stogumber,' Gently said.

The man inspected him with an amused eye. He wiped his hands on his baize apron.

'Mr Stogumber isn't in,' he said.

Gently hesitated. 'Where shall I find him?'

'You'll find him out here,' the man said. 'Talking to two policemen. One of whom doesn't know Jimmy Stogumber.' He chuckled and pushed out an earthy hand. 'Don't bother with introductions,' he said. 'My

70

daughter was over here this afternoon, so I've heard all about you.'

Gently shook hands. Stogumber stood smiling. He was a fine-looking man in his seventies. He'd lost none of his cropped, grizzled hair, and he carried a strong body with little stoop. But there was tired flesh about his face and tired lines around his eyes. He was wearing decrepit flannel trousers and, in spite of the heat, a knitted pullover.

'Yes, you upset my Marie,' he said. 'Her opinion of policemen is rather low just now. And she's right, you know. Poor Charles did reform. I'll be surprised myself if there's another woman in it.'

'This will have been a big shock to you,' Gently said.

'Yes, it's a sad business,' Stogumber said. 'But here I am keeping you standing in the sun. Let's go inside and talk there.'

He gestured courteously, and stood aside for Gently and Docking to precede him into the house. They went up an apron of brick steps, planted each side with chalk-blue hydrangeas, and passed through a spacious doorway, with a carved lintel, into a panelled hall with a pemmon floor. An oak staircase rose on the right to a gallery at first-floor level. Darkened portraits in oils ranged down the wall on the left. The pemmons were covered with woven rush matting, fragrant, yielding underfoot, and at the end of the hall, beneath the gallery, spread a wide, stone-shafted window.

'All in the family,' Stogumber said, waving a hand at the portraits. 'The one at the end is old Aylmer Stogumber, who sailed with Drake and married an heiress. The family was Devonshire in those days, but

Aylmer came this way when he married.' He smiled. 'We're still foreigners, of course. We've only been here four centuries.'

'So your son is last of the line,' Gently said.

'Yes,' Stogumber said. 'The last with the name. There's Leo, of course, and Marie's expecting, but Lachlan's the only one with the name.'

'No doubt he'll hand it on . . . ?'

Stogumber clicked his tongue. 'I sometimes wonder if I shall see the day. But he's twenty-two, so there's time yet. Though he'll need another mistress besides the muse.'

He pushed open a door and ushered them into a long, low-ceilinged room with mullioned lattice-windows. It was furnished discreetly with a mixture of period pieces and of more comfortable modern furniture.

'Sit you down while I rinse these hands.'

When he returned, he brought a tray of drinks with him. He handed them round with grave politeness, then carried his own to a high settle by the windows. He sat, resting one leg along the settle.

'Now, gentlemen, we can get to business. But if you've come here hoping I can name the woman for you, then I'm afraid I must disappoint you.'

Gently shook his head. 'That wasn't the object. Though, naturally, I value your opinion.'

'And I gave it to you,' Stogumber said. 'I doubt whether this woman ever existed. Heaven knows, I wasn't in favour of Marie's wedding, but one must give the devil his due. Charles was infatuated with Marie. Let me define what I mean by that. A man is infatuated with a woman when he is in love and she isn't. And that's

72

how it was with Charles and Marie: he loved her, and she let him.' He dropped his eyes from Gently's. 'She's a wilful girl. I'm afraid her marriage was just an act of rebellion.'

'Against you?' Gently said.

Stogumber nodded. 'Mine are a pair of sad children,' he said. 'They lacked their mother. She died with Marie. Poor Stella. She was never a strong one.'

'But your daughter must have had some fondness for Berney,' Gently said.

'Aye, well . . . in her way,' Stogumber admitted. 'But it blew up suddenly on the tail of a row. I can never get that out of my mind. Charles would always hang around Marie, but Marie knew well enough how to snub him. Then there was a scene at quarter-day about Marie's allowance, and after that she turned right round.'

'Are you suggesting it was his money?'

'No, no,' Stogumber said. 'I know Marie better than that. She was wanting to slip an old father she couldn't manage, to take on a husband who she could.' He gave a little sigh. 'And she knew the way,' he said. 'One look at her must have told you that.'

'What was her brother's reaction?' Gently asked.

Stogumber's hand twitched. 'He backed her up. Lachlan will always back up Marie, and she him, against me.'

'And your cousin?'

'Leo's neutral . . . perhaps a little on the old man's side. But that's no good. Against Lachlan and Marie, we might as well hold our peace.'

Gently sipped some of his drink (it was ice-cold bitter). 'So you don't favour the police theory,' he said.

'It wasn't a woman who lured Berney on the heath. Perhaps you have an idea who did?'

Stogumber frowned at his blotched hands. 'I haven't,' he said. 'It's a mystery to me. Charles's actions on Tuesday make no sort of sense. It's as though he went fey, was expecting death.'

'I think there was a reason,' Gently said.

'Yes, that's your business,' Stogumber agreed. 'But I'm an old man, I remember things. This reminds me very much of my father's death.'

Gently stared. 'Was he killed by a horse?'

Stogumber shook his head. 'He gassed himself. But there's the point. One day he went off, with no imaginable reason, booked a room in a hotel, and turned on the gas. Till then he was a normal, sane person. You couldn't have guessed he'd do any such thing. No troubles with money, health or women. Yet suddenly he went fey and took his life.'

'But that's all the connection,' Gently shrugged.

'It's the best I can do,' Stogumber replied. 'Just like my father, Charles went off on Tuesday, did inexplicable things, and died.'

'Only,' Gently said, 'in this case there was a horse. And horses you don't simply turn on.'

Stogumber's tired eyes lifted. 'Have you found the horse?'

Gently nodded. 'It was Farmer Creke's.'

'Farmer Creke's!' Stogumber echoed, his eyes widening, searching into Gently's. 'But . . . can you be sure?'

'Fairly sure,' Gently said. 'His horse would have been available on Tuesday.'

'Oh my goodness!' Stogumber exclaimed.

'Is it really a surprise to you?' Gently said.

Stogumber shook his head dumbly, his lips trembling. The beer was slopping in his glass.

'This is a shock, truly a shock. Oh my goodness, poor Charles! Of course, I've wondered about the horse, but I wouldn't let myself think it was that one.' He set the shaking glass on the settle. 'You will have seen Creke?' he said.

'We've seen him.'

'It wasn't . . . him?'

'Creke has an alibi,' Gently said.

'Thank heaven,' Stogumber said. 'I couldn't have taken that. Not my own tenant the guilty man.' His face twisted and he pressed his hand to his chest. 'Sorry,' he said. 'Sorry, but it's a shock.'

Gently paused, watching him. 'Are you all right, sir?'

'Yes, yes, I'm all right,' Stogumber said.

'If you'd sooner we went—'

'No, stay. It's my cursed heart. But I'm all right.'

A little grey-faced, he picked up the glass and took two or three firm swigs. Then he returned the glass to the seat and faced Gently again.

'That terrible horse! I had a premonition it would do some harm one day. I warned Creke, but he would never listen. Now he'll have to put it down.'

'You're familiar with the horse,' Gently said.

'I've seen it once or twice,' Stogumber said. 'We've always been horse people in this family. We can never resist looking at a horse.'

'Have you ever ridden him?'

Stogumber forced a smile. 'I'm afraid he's out of my class these days.'

'Have you seen him ridden?'

'I've seen Creke on him. He's like a lamb with Creke up.'

Gently studied his glass for a moment. 'I think you'll appreciate the position,' he said. 'We've found the horse, now we have to find the rider. And we can only do that by elimination.'

Stogumber faltered. 'Couldn't Creke tell you that?'

Gently shook his head. 'Creke couldn't. Or wouldn't.'

'Well then . . . may I take it I'm eliminated?'

'I'd sooner,' Gently said, 'that you didn't.'

Stogumber looked aslant, his hand straying to his chest. 'This is a strange state of affairs,' he said. 'Good heavens, I never thought it would come to this, with me being suspected of killing my own son-in-law.' He pressed his chest. 'But that's your affair. Let it never be said that I obstructed your inquiry. On Tuesday afternoon I was in the kitchen garden. I was burning pea haulms and generally pottering.'

'Have you a witness?' Gently said.

'No, I don't have a witness. Tuesday isn't one of Johnson's days. But truthfully, I could never have saddled and ridden that stallion. Jerry Rising's old cob is all I aspire to.'

Gently nodded deliberately. 'I'll accept that,' he said. 'But couldn't your son have been your witness?'

'Lachlan,' Stogumber said. 'He was writing in his study. I might have gone to the moon for all he'd notice.'

'Well, your cousin,' Gently said.

'He's a bug-hunter. He went out after breakfast.'

'Went where?'

'To Stukey Woods,' said a voice by the door. 'In search of *Orchis hircina*. May I come in?'

He had opened the door very silently: a tall, ruddy-faced man of around fifty, clad in a bush-shirt with buttoned pockets and carrying binoculars slung from his shoulder. He smiled ingratiatingly. He had smooth, regular features and unassuming hazel eyes. Along with the binoculars hung a botanical collecting canister, and from one of his pockets sprouted an array of ball-pens.

'I'm the bug-hunter,' he smiled. 'Cousin Leo. I saw your magnificent beast parked outside. White, and fitted with R/T. I knew the gendarmerie must be with us.'

'I see,' Gently said. 'Have you just come in?'

'Just this moment,' Leo Redmayne smiled. 'I've been in the back woods, towards Clayfield. Still searching for the elusive *Orchis hircina*.'

'It must be quite an attraction,' Gently said.

'Oh, it would be a feather in my cap if I found one,' Redmayne smiled. 'But it wouldn't make a brilliant alibi, would it? And I gather that's the object of the present visit.'

'They've identified the horse, Leo,' Stogumber said.

'Have they?' Redmayne said. 'That's a step forward. Whose was it?'

'It was Creke's. But Nat wasn't riding it at the time.'

Redmayne made a mouth. He looked around, dumped his binoculars and canister in a chair. Then he came forward to the settle. Stogumber shifted his leg, and Redmayne sat.

'So now it's alibis,' he said. 'Every soul who rides a

horse.' He grinned at Gently. 'I'm a sitting duck,' he said. 'I didn't even find my *Orchis hircina*.'

'Where are Stukey Woods?' Gently asked Docking.

'Going towards Welling, sir,' Docking said. 'That's beyond Clayfield, about seven miles. Quite a big area of woods there, sir.'

'And not a soul in them,' Redmayne smiled. 'And no special permission from Sir Thomas Booke, who owns them. As an alibi it's so hopeless that you're almost compelled to believe it.'

Gently gave him a quick stare. 'You drove there?'

'Yes – but that was mid-morning.'

'You'd park your car somewhere?'

'At the lodge cottage. But that's no good either – it's empty.'

'What make is your car?'

'A Renault 4L. The first truly modern car. You can see it yourself in the coach-house – lots of mud, but no blood.'

'Leo didn't get back till tea,' Stogumber said. 'And I saw him come in from Clayfield way.'

'Ah, but that was at five-thirty, Jimmy,' Redmayne said. 'I'd have had time to circle back there and arrive all innocent. No, you can't spoil my non-alibi. It would stand up in the courts anywhere.' He smiled pleasantly at Gently. 'Opportunity,' he said. 'But utterly no motive. Charles was a good friend of mine, and Marie is my favourite second cousin.'

Gently stayed poker-faced. 'And of course, you're not a poet?'

Redmayne looked surprised. 'Would it be against me?'

'Oh, there's some nonsense about one of Lachlan's poems,' Stogumber said impatiently. 'Marie was over this afternoon and told us about it.'

'One of Lachlan's poems,' Redmayne said slowly. 'I wonder how that came into the case. Lachlan shows everything he writes to Marie, but it wasn't an interest that Charlie shared.'

'Perhaps you'd answer my question,' Gently said.

Redmayne laughed. 'I don't know,' he said. 'Suddenly, you've made it all seem very sinister, as though you were laying one of your famous traps.' He tapped his fingers on the seat of the settle. 'Very well, then,' he said. 'I'll play. When I was young and foolish I published one of those slim volumes.'

'Good heavens!' Stogumber said. 'I never knew that, Leo.'

'I've taken good care you shouldn't,' Redmayne smiled. 'In this high temple of Apollo I wouldn't care to admit my indiscretions.'

'You wrote traditional verse,' Gently said. 'Sonnets?'

'That's between me and God,' Redmayne said. 'It was thirty years ago, near enough. I'm hoping my trespasses have been forgiven. Anyway, what's the score?'

Gently shook his head. 'Have you ever ridden Creke's stallion?' he asked.

'That sounds even more sinister,' Redmayne said. 'If I admitted it, would you arrest me?'

'Have you?'

Redmayne shrugged. 'Once.'

'By George,' Stogumber said. 'Did you stay on, Leo?'

'About five bucks,' Redmayne grimaced. 'It may have been six. Creke was laughing like a hyena.'

'And it was just that once?' Gently said.

'Just that once,' Redmayne said. He paused. 'Didn't Creke tell you?'

Gently stared at him, said nothing.

Redmayne's fingers tapped the settle again. 'I don't think this is getting you anywhere,' he said. 'You've had a guess at the horse — it was a guess, wasn't it? But that doesn't give you a man or a motive. All you've got is Charles acting the goat, and getting himself savaged on the heath. Well, he married a Stogumber. Perhaps that's as much explanation as you need.'

Gently looked at him woodenly. 'Is this a theory?'

'Say a comment in passing,' Redmayne said. 'There's a Stogumber family curse, and part of it may have rubbed off on Charles.'

'Go on,' Gently said.

'Well, according to the curse, we either live unhappily or die unnaturally. And Charles was living the life of Riley, so he'd be bound to end badly.'

Gently nodded. 'And is your life a happy one?'

'I'm only a cousin,' Redmayne smiled. 'But some of my books have had stinking reviews, and if there's justice, that should clear me.'

Stogumber's hand moved to his chest. 'My father was a happy man,' he said. 'But I think I've worn the curse out. There can't be much claim on me now.'

Redmayne patted his cousin's arm. Stogumber slowly rose to his feet.

'Perhaps you'll excuse me, gentlemen,' he said. 'I have to tidy myself for tea.'

'That goes for me too,' Redmayne said. 'Unless you have some other thrilling questions.'

'No,' Gently said. 'Not just now. But I've one or two to ask Lachlan Stogumber.'

Redmayne hesitated very slightly, then his smile renewed itself. He rose. 'I'll take you to his study,' he said. 'He won't be pleased to see you, but you mustn't expect graciousness when you meet a poet.'

CHAPTER SEVEN

A FAINT ODOUR of roasting meat was penetrating the
hall as they re-entered it. Redmayne checked his
step to sniff appraisingly, then he caught Gently's eye
and winked.

'One of Lottie's mixed grills, or I'm much mistaken.
A pity you're not staying for a meal.'

'Lottie . . . ?'

'Charlotte Greengrass, our housekeeper. She's been at
the Manor since Jimmy's wife died.'

'She lives in, of course.'

Redmayne's smile was broad. 'Yes, but Lottie will be
no help to you. Tuesday is her day off, and one of us
runs her into Hale. Our other two domestics come only
mornings, and Tuesday isn't the gardener's day. Alibis
are the devil in the country.'

'How many cars have you here?' Gently asked.

'One each. Mine, you know about. Lachlan has a
TR4. Jimmy still runs his old Armstrong-Siddeley.' He
raised an eyebrow at Gently. 'Pass?'

Gently grunted, motioned him to lead on.

* * *

They ascended to the gallery. It formed part of a corridor running the entire length of the house, fairly straight, but with changes of level that required a step or two here and there. Small windows overlooked neat kitchen gardens, orchards, a greenhouse and a backing of tall trees. The inner walls were pierced with panelled oak doors and hung with early nineteenth-century water colours and county maps.

Redmayne turned right and proceeded along the corridor to a facing door at the end. He tapped softly, hesitated, then half opened the door and put his head round it.

'Her Majesty's Servants are here, Lachlan,' he said. 'They think it was Nat's horse that killed Charlie. Now they want alibis from all horse-riders . . . is it all right to show them in?'

Gently pushed past him into the room.

'Chief Superintendent Gently,' he said.

A tall young man rose from a desk by the window. He drew himself up to his full height: he gazed at Gently.

The room was a wing-room, well proportioned, and panelled throughout with linen-fold panelling. At the front it had a fine bay window with mullioned lattices and window seats. Smaller windows on two other walls broke up rows of natural oak bookcases, and the desk, chairs and a low table were constructed of similar wood. The floor, polished but unstained, was laid with the same rush matting as the hall. The ceiling was of moulded plaster, in a floral pattern, enriched with bosses and heavily corniced.

The young man moved his chair aside. He was slim,

and athletic in his motions. He had the same smooth symmetry of feature as his sister, but his hair, worn medium long, had a reddish tint. Like Redmayne, he had hazel eyes, but they were golden-hazel, large and brilliant. Between the three of them was a strong family resemblance, more marked than the resemblance they shared with James Stogumber.

'So you are the man,' Lachlan Stogumber said cuttingly. 'My sister has been telling me about you. I suppose the fact that she has suffered a personal tragedy gives you every right to annoy her.'

'Oh, come now, Lachlan,' Redmayne said. 'These people have to ask their questions.'

'But they don't have to be offensive,' Lachlan Stogumber said. 'And if they had intelligence enough they wouldn't need to be.'

Redmayne chuckled. 'You'd better let them off lightly. I think they're trying to make bricks without straw. And Lottie's preparing a mixed grill for tea, so' – he made a mocking little bow to Gently – 'the sooner you get shut of them, the better.'

Lachlan Stogumber eyed his relative disdainfully. Then he threw down the pencil he'd been holding.

'Sit down, gentlemen,' he said. 'We pay rates for something, even if it's to have our time wasted.'

Redmayne grinned at Gently, lingered a moment, then quietly slipped out of the room. Lachlan Stogumber closed a manuscript book that lay open on the desk, turned his chair, and sat. Docking sat modestly by the books. Gently sauntered forward to the desk. He shoved aside some books and papers and sat on the desk, looking down at the poet.

'Please be comfortable,' Lachlan Stogumber said icily.

'Thanks,' Gently said. He picked up the pencil. 'Is this your usual weapon?'

'Is that a relevant question?'

Gently shook his head. 'Just curious about poets.'

Lachlan Stogumber's stare was withering. 'I don't have time for your curiosity,' he said. 'If you have questions to ask, please ask them. I understand you're checking our movements on Tuesday.'

'Just routine,' Gently said. 'Completing the picture. It isn't really very important.' He took a sight along the pencil. 'But something you can tell me. Why did your sister marry Berney?'

Lachlan Stogumber's head drew back. 'Is it any concern of yours?' he said. 'What my sister does is her own business. She doesn't have to account for her actions to you.'

'Still, it's unusual,' Gently said. 'A lively and beautiful girl like Marie. And a fellow like Berney, old enough to be her father – a man she'd known since she was a child.'

Lachlan Stogumber laughed scornfully. 'A pity you're so ignorant of human nature. You think that because Marie is regal and beautiful she'd be interested only in the young men. But that's precisely the point. She was out of their class. They were too stupid and raw to attract her. It needed a mature, experienced man – one with intelligence, with reverence.'

'And that describes Berney?' Gently said.

'Yes. Charles was the right person for Marie.'

'In spite of his flaws?'

'All that was in the past. Marie made a condition about that when she accepted him.'

'A condition,' Gently said. He twirled the pencil. 'People who make conditions usually bargain from strength.'

'And so Marie did,' Lachlan Stogumber said. 'Charles was dementedly in love with her.'

'But she . . . rather less?' Gently suggested.

Lachlan Stogumber gave him a fleering look.

'You see what I'm driving at,' Gently said. 'Berney was obviously put on his best behaviour. He was on parole, you might say, he had to be more careful than the ordinary citizen. One slip, and presumably your sister would have filed suit against him. Yet though he loved your sister, the spots ran deep. And he still had his old contacts.'

'But he didn't,' Lachlan Stogumber said. 'That's where you're so pig-headed. It was all over — a clean sweep.'

'Was it all over on Monday night?'

'Yes – in spite of your impounding one of my poems!' Gently held up the pencil between them. 'Presumably,' he said, 'this is for first drafts?'

Lachlan Stogumber's eyes flamed for a second; then he slewed in his chair to pull open a desk drawer. He lifted from it an Olympia typewriter and placed it on the desk beside Gently. He sat back. Gently reached for a sheet of paper, fed it in and tapped a few keys. The same distinctive, italic type that the sonnet was typed in appeared on the paper. And the paper was the same. An opened packet of it lay on the table, among other clutter.

'Perhaps now you'll be convinced?'

Lachlan Stogumber was watching him mockingly. Gently took from his wallet the sonnet and another piece of folded paper. He spread them on the desk.

'There – your latest published poem. And the sonnet your sister took from her husband. Two poems . . . but only one poet?'

'Yes – one poet!'

Lachlan Stogumber started up from his chair. His eyes glinted: he stared down at Gently with a fierce, hawk-like expression.

'I wrote them both. Who else? Who else in the world can write this poetry? Show me another man writing like this. Show me another man who dare.'

Gently shrugged. 'I'd say there was a century between your poem and the other.'

'A century – more than a century! And yet both the poems are mine.'

'You write pastiche?'

'It isn't pastiche.'

'It isn't what the *New Statesman* is using.'

'But it isn't pastiche. This is the New Wave, the post-anarchy, the second renaissance.'

Gently stared. 'That's new to me. I thought there was just Betjeman and the others.'

'Betjeman! Betjeman is a Georgian hangover.'

'A traditionalist.'

'Yes. But before the flood.'

Lachlan Stogumber took some steps about the room. There was a flush in his face and his eyes were aglitter. His soft, fine hair, with its auburn lights, tumbled forward about his brow and cheeks. He came back to the desk and pointed dramatically at the poem clipped from the *New Statesman*.

'Keep that. It's a literary watershed. At that point I turned my back on anarchy. That's what the old mole was digging out of chaos. I shall never write like that again.'

'But surely this is the current idiom?' Gently said.

Lachlan Stogumber shook his head vigorously. 'It's the past, the dark past, part of the long night of anarchy. Oh, it was necessary. Poetry was sick, it had been in decay since the Romantics. It needed anarchy, blasphemy, atheism, a great roll in its own vomit. But now it's had it. Now the patient is stirring, ready to get up from his bed.' He touched the clipping. 'You can still smell the vomit.' He touched the sonnet. 'But also, fresh air.'

'I see,' Gently said. 'I seem to have called at a historic moment.'

'Anarchy is dead,' Lachlan Stogumber said. 'To be a poet now, one must write poetry. Thomas was the only poet of the Abyss, and the Abyss crushed him with its darkness. It was eighteen straight sonnets, not straight whiskies, that poisoned Dylan.'

'An interesting theory,' Gently said. 'And so, in a flash of vision, you've turned traditionalist.'

'If that's a label you understand,' Lachlan Stogumber said scornfully. 'Yes. I'm beginning again at the Piazza di Spagna.'

'Where Keats died,' Gently said. 'But I can think of another reason why an inarticulate poet should suddenly want to be articulate, and it has nothing to do with

88

historic necessity.' He laid a finger on the sonnet. 'He could fall in love.'

Lachlan Stogumber's eyes raked him. 'Clever,' he said. 'You're so clever. Even you have intelligence enough to identify that as a love-poem.'

'Did you write it?'

'Prove otherwise!'

'I'll have a try,' Gently said. He picked up the sonnet. 'Type me a copy,' he said. 'I'll need one anyway, for comparison.'

Lachlan Stogumber didn't move.

'Come on,' Gently said. 'Type me a copy.'

'You know I can't, don't you?' Lachlan Stogumber said bitterly. 'One doesn't remember them as precisely as that.'

'You don't remember your own poem?'

'No – not a poem like the sonnet! It's the sort that comes out like a bud expanding, you don't know how, and you don't remember. There's another sort, the sort you labour at, and come back to, and work over – those you remember. But even those you may not recall in exact detail.'

Gently shrugged. 'One's always learning! But I'll still need a copy.'

'Give me the one you have, then.'

'I suggest you use the original draft.'

Lachlan Stogumber eyed him steadily. 'It isn't convenient to use it,' he said. 'And I don't intend to produce it for you. So give me that one, or go without.'

'You do want me to accept that the poem is yours?'

'As I said before – prove otherwise.'

Their eyes linked tightly for a moment, then Gently

slowly shook his head. He laid the sonnet on the desk beside the typewriter. Lachlan Stogumber sat down and fed in fresh paper.

Gently rose, moved round the desk, stood staring through the spreading, many-paned windows. Below was the gravel sweep, then smooth-shaven lawns, separated from the drive by the moulded yew hedges. Across the road was a rough paddock and a line of seven black poplars. Then the heath began. In dark, heat-hazed ridges it stretched far off, with the sky bleached behind it.

'So let's suppose the poem's yours,' Gently said, without turning. Behind him the patter of the type-writer hesitated. 'A poem you wrote – like a bud expanding – to a woman you apparently can't visit very freely. You wouldn't tell me her name?'

There was a brief silence. 'I'll leave you to guess,' Lachlan Stogumber said tartly.

Gently nodded to the window. 'I'll be happy to do that. My guess is she lives just across the heath.' He waited. Lachlan Stogumber said nothing. 'Yes, across the heath,' Gently continued. 'And sometimes her occasions would take her on the heath – perhaps bring her in sight of this window. She's a handsome woman, tallish, fine-figured, and you're probably not the first to be smitten by her. Someone else may have had his eye on her, this handsome woman who frequented the heath.' He turned from the window. 'Am I right?'

Lachlan Stogumber was staring at him fiercely. There was paleness in the young man's cheek and his full-lipped mouth was drawn small.

'You're doing the guessing,' he said aggressively.

90

'Let's say I'm guessing right,' Gently said. 'And I'm guessing the other man was Charles Berney – and that Monday's party put him wise.'

'You don't know that.'

Gently pointed to the sonnet. 'That's what made the penny drop. Somehow it got into Berney's hands, and it was no riddle to him.'

'He didn't read it. Marie got it away from him.'

'I think he read enough,' Gently said. He paused. 'You still want to claim it as yours?'

Lachlan Stogumber's eyes flamed at him.

'Take it from there, and it's simple,' Gently said. 'Berney decided he would interrupt things. He surprised you and the lady on the heath, and somehow he got himself under a horse. Of course, you have an alibi – you were up here writing – but I know already that you can't confirm it. And in the matter of horses, there's Farmer Creke's stallion, while presumably the lady herself was mounted.'

Something clicked in Lachlan Stogumber's stare. His face loosened, he began to smile.

'Clever,' he said. 'And now all I have to do is break down and admit that Charlie wrote the sonnet.'

Gently nodded, watching him. 'Something like that.'

'Exactly like that – or it's no use to you. If Charlie didn't write it you're back to square one – making up fables about mystery ladies.'

'Is the lady such a mystery?'

Lachlan Stogumber laughed tauntingly. 'She isn't the one you've tried to saddle me with. And for all you know she doesn't exist – I may just have been trying my hand at a love sonnet.' He began typing again, striking the keys jauntily. 'I should forget the stallion too,' he said. 'If you've seen it, you'll know that only Nat can ride it. If Nat didn't kill Charles, we don't need alibis.'

'Mr Redmayne has ridden the stallion,' Gently said.

'Leo? Don't believe all he tells you.'

'What are you telling me?'

Lachlan Stogumber laughed again. 'The truth. It's what poets are famous for.'

He finished the typing with a flourish and handed the poem and the copy to Gently. Gently made a quick comparison of the two typescripts. There was little doubt they were a match. Lachlan Stogumber spread his hands.

'Final proof. Now you'll be happy.'

Gently shrugged and folded away the sheets. Docking, in the background, was easing to his feet.

'Perhaps you haven't solved much,' Lachlan Stogumber grinned. But you've had your fun – and you've met a poet.'

He mockingly offered his hand to Gently.

Gently stared past him, didn't take it.

Outside the study they found Redmayne lounging casually by a window. He put his finger to his lips while Docking closed the heavy door. Gently flung him a look.

'Could you hear everything?'

Redmayne smiled, unoffended. 'Pretty well everything. Though, naturally, I missed the revealing interplay of expressions.' He fell into step beside Gently. 'I thought the Wonderful Boy was exercising restraint. He

92

can throw some brilliant temperament when he wants to. I'd say he must have taken a shine to you.'

Gently grunted. They came to the stairs.

'I adored your theory,' Redmayne said, keeping close. 'Of course, you wouldn't know it, but your reasoning falls flat on one very important point. Lachlan has never shown much interest in the ladies. He doesn't chase them or encourage them. According to my observation his only love is the muse – in fact, I'd lay a cool hundred that Lachlan is a virgin.'

Gently crossed the hall. He didn't look back.

'I see,' Redmayne said. 'You don't take my word. But I'm a trained observer too, just like yourself, and I'm in an exceptional position to report on this subject. You'd be a fool to ignore that.'

At the top of the brick steps, Gently swung on him. 'A trained observer! So what did the trained observer see at Berney's party?'

'At Charlie's party . . . ?' Redmayne's eyes were wary. 'What am I supposed to say to that?'

'You were there.'

'Freely admitted. But I don't see anything that you might call significant.'

'Not some business with that poem?'

Redmayne shook his head.

'Nothing?'

'Not that I remember.' He stared back at Gently, his eyes blank.

'Yet something significant did happen,' Gently said. 'And a trained observer might have seen it. Should have, would have seen it – ought to be able to report on it now. Straight after that party Berney began to act

93

queerly and his actions terminated in his death. But you saw nothing, heard nothing – didn't even notice a change of expression?'

Redmayne shook his head again. 'Sorry and all that.'

'Come on!' Gently said to Docking.

They went down the steps and got in the car. Redmayne stayed where they had left him.

CHAPTER EIGHT

THE SUN WAS sloping as the Lotus fizzed its way back to Low Hale and Gently, driving towards it, was glad to pull down his vizor. Cars and cyclists were heading out of town and girls were clustering at a bus-stop. An icecream van, pulled in near the police station, was doing brisk trade with home-going workers.

Docking took Gently to his own office, a small room facing the M/T yard. Waters, one of the Detective Constables, sat at a table typing his report.

'Don't get up,' Gently said.

Waters, half-up, sank on his chair again. He was a red-faced, thick-featured young man with a benignly innocent expression.

'Haven't had a lot of luck, sir,' he said. 'Don't think the others have either.' He pointed to a couple of report sheets which were lying on Docking's desk.

'Where's Bayfield now?' Docking asked.

'He's gone out to Hanworth, sir. The chummies have been on the church roof – stripped it clean, so the local man says.'

Docking humphed. He unlocked a filing-cabinet and produced three squat brown bottles. He looked around. Waters dived into his pocket, handed Docking a knife that comprised a bottle-opener.

Gently sat down at Docking's desk and glanced over the two report sheets. They were scantly filled. Dr Pleasants now had the perfect alibi of a difficult confinement. Bayfield, who must have travelled many hot miles, had added three more horses to the list, but they were stabled rather distant from High Hale heath and their security was sworn to by their owners. No horsebox or cattle-float had been noticed in the village on Tuesday, and nobody except Mrs Bircham had seen a rider on the heath.

Waters's stint had been Starmouth, and he had succeeded in filling two minor gaps. About five miles out of the town, on the coast road, he had found the café that had supplied Berney with coffee and sandwiches. It was the car which the café-proprietor chiefly remembered – Berney had driven a puce Jaguar XJ6 – but he recalled that the customer had been wearing a lightweight grey linen jacket; and so had Berney when he died.

'Could he fix the time?' Gently asked.

'Reckoned it was soon after ten, sir,' Waters said. 'That would square with Berney's driving straight back there. He left the Britannic in Starmouth at about ten.'

'Did he seem in a hurry?'

'I asked that, sir, but my man didn't particularly notice.'

'He was alone, was he?'

'Yes, sir. The man had his eye on the car.'

Waters's other contribution was a sighting of the car at a coast-road village ten miles from High Hale. His informant there was a filling-station attendant who had also been struck by the distinctive mark and colour. Also the car had been travelling fast: it had hit the bend near the filling-station with squealing tyres. The informant was uncertain about the time, putting it somewhere about mid-morning.

'Sounds as though he did come straight back, sir,' Docking said. 'He wanted to get into cover before he was spotted.'

Gently brooded over his pipe. 'But why?' he said. 'The lies . . . the hotel room . . . the long wait?'

Docking pulled up the visitor's chair and sat, stretching his long legs straight in front of him 'I don't know, sir,' he said. 'You've put up a couple of theories, but I reckon the second one fits best.'

Gently nostrilled smoke. 'Carry on,' he said.

'Well, sir,' Docking said. 'This bit about the poem. There's nothing on it to say who it's written to, so even if Berney guessed he could hardly have used it for blackmail. But if he did guess, it could put him in the way of it. He had only to catch young Stogumber and Mrs Rising together. So somehow he figured they were meeting on Tuesday, and he set it up and laid in wait for them.'

Gently puffed. 'Do you have a map?'

'Yes, sir.' Docking climbed to his feet again and went to the filing-cabinet. He brought a two-and-a-half-inch O.S. map and spread it on the desk in front of Gently. It took in the complete section of coast with Low Hale down in the right-hand corner. To the left was

Clayfield, at the centre top High Hale, in the middle the long run of the heath.

'Mark it up – where the body was found, where Berney concealed his car.'

Docking took a red pencil from the desk tray and deftly applied two crosses.

Gently shrugged. 'There's your answer. Berney was in the wrong part of the heath. In fact, the body was found in the wrong path of the heath. It's way off the line between Clayfield and the Manor.'

'Yes, but just a minute, sir,' Docking said. 'We don't know how much Berney knew. He might have overheard something, the time, the place. He must have been pretty certain they were meeting on Tuesday.'

'Seems a lot to overhear,' Gently said. 'And the trysting-place is still a long way from Clayfield.' He trailed a finger across the map. 'It's more on the line from High Hale village.'

'But, sir – that's just right!' Docking faced him excitedly. 'Remember, she let on she was picking up the kids from school. Well, there isn't a school at Clayfield. The kids from there go to Hale.'

'So?' Gently said.

'She came over in the car, sir, so she'd have it there to pick up the kids later. Then she took the car up on the heath and walked across to the valley to meet Stogumber.'

'With Berney right on the spot to follow her.'

'Yes, sir. She'd have to drive at a crawl, on the heath.'

'Berney,' Gently said, 'being psychic, and thus knowing Mrs Rising would come that way.'

Docking coloured. 'I don't know about that, sir. But

Berney must have heard something. He got the day right. He wouldn't have done what he did just on the chance of something happening.'

'Unless ... somehow ... he knew he was on a certainty.'

'Don't see how he could have guessed about it, sir.'

'And I don't see how he could have come by the information,' Gently said. 'Unless, of course, someone told him.' He puffed a little, then shook his head. 'There are too many loopholes,' he said. 'If Mrs Rising was using a car, why bother to go on the heath at all?' He pointed to the map. 'Look – that road to the Manor. It keeps on westward, at the back of the heaths. Then it's joined by this track coming down from Clayfield ... impossible to get a car along there? She could have picked up Stogumber, or he her, and then gone off in the woods somewhere. I'd say they were a better prospect for lovers in this sort of weather.'

'She had to be at the village by a quarter to four, sir.'

Gently shrugged. 'Not much of a problem! The point is that she needn't have come on the heath if she were driving, and if she were riding there were nearer places to meet Stogumber.'

'Perhaps there were special reasons for this place,' Docking said.

'Perhaps,' Gently said. 'Make a suggestion.'

Docking stared resentfully at the map for some moments, then sighed and tilted his brown bottle. Waters, who'd finished his bottle a while back, edged closer to the desk for a glimpse of the map.

'Sir, it'd be the right place for Berney to meet her,' he ventured. 'If we know the woman was Mrs Rising.'

Gently favoured him with a small smoke-ring. 'We're not even sure of that,' he said. 'Which brings us back to square one, as Mr Lachlan Stogumber predicted. Berney wrote the poem, made the assignation, was surprised by the injured husband. With the addition that his wife certainly knew about it – which means she may have passed on the information.' He looked from Waters to Docking. 'Any advance?'

Waters looked blank. Docking shook his head.

'Three theories,' Gently puffed. 'And we don't like any of them . . . as though somehow we'd got on a wrong track.'

Docking cleared his throat. 'It comes back to this, sir. There's a woman in the case, and we've got to nab her. If she isn't Mrs Rising, we've got to prove that, and then start looking elsewhere.'

'Find the woman . . . !'

'Yes, sir. And I'm pretty sure in my own mind that we've found her.'

Gently smiled up at him through wreaths of smoke. 'Right,' he said. 'We'll work on that.'

He left Docking waiting for a report on the lead theft and drove to the Royal William for a shower and dinner. The hotel had a busy air. Its rather small yard was packed with Capris, Ventoras and similar vehicles. In the soft-lit dining-room, barricaded in a corner, a trio was playing a selection from The Arcadians, and sweat shone beneath the powder of the waitresses as they hastened between the tables and the swing doors to the kitchen. The manager was on the look-out for Gently. He was a plump, jowled man with a toper's complexion.

He ushered Gently ostentatiously to his table and hung about while the waitress took the order.

'Was your room satisfactory . . . everything all right?'

He seemed to be angling for a chance to talk. At last he retired to a small table by the wall, where sat a smartly dressed woman, doubtless his wife.

The music played, and Gently ate, but the manager's officiousness had done its job. Eyes were perpetually turning to him from other tables; voices were lowered, there were nervous laughs.

The manager also kept staring uneasily, sometimes with his fork half-way to his mouth. His wife, on the other hand, paid no attention, either to Gently or the manager. She was sharply good-looking, perhaps part-Jewish, and ate her food with an air.

'Fruit salad or trifle, sir?'

'I'll have the fruit salad.'

On another table, two couples were eyeing him silently. One of the men was flush-faced and severe-looking. The other had horsey features and a pronounced Adam's apple.

'Cream, sir?'

Gently nodded. 'You have a full house tonight,' he said.

The waitress flashed him a smile. 'It's a Friday night, sir. We always get them in at the weekend.'

'Who are those people by the window?'

'That's our town clerk, sir, the serious one. Mr Wade. And Mr Drury, he's the auctioneer and estate agent.'

'With their wives?'

'Yes − of course, sir!' The waitress sounded quite indignant.

Gently smiled to himself. Not much doubt about what was in the minds of Messrs Wade and Drury! However delicate Docking's probing had been, they must have had an idea of which way the wind blew. And now they sat vulnerable, under Gently's eye, each with his frail vessel beside him: on pins in case he should saunter across and begin again where Docking left off . . .

Covertly, Gently studied the two women, a trendy-looking blonde and a fulsome brunette. The latter had her back to him, but when she leaned forward she revealed shapely hips and a weight of bosom. The blonde was taller, firmer, twiggier, and wore her hair in an elaborate set. She caught Gently's eye, and her eyes went large; then Wade snapped something and she looked away sulkily.

A handful there!

But would Berney have been the first one? Somehow, you got the impression that Wade had learned to live with it.

Drury, by contrast, looked a man who might bear a grudge; a tall, stringy fellow with a long, hectoring face. Also, Drury was a horseman and a patron of the Rising stable . . . but he had a foolproof alibi, Gently recalled: Tuesday was sale-day at Low Hale.

No . . . on balance, he'd leave the Wades and Drurys to digest their dinner . . .

'Where would you like your coffee, sir?'

Gently hesitated. 'Is there somewhere private?'

'There's the Little Lounge, sir. Not many people go in there.'

'Bring it to me there, then.'

He was tired of being the centre of attention! On the way out, he glanced at Mrs Drury. She had a pretty face, but foolish eyes.

In the Little Lounge he disturbed a couple who'd been necking on the settee, but after a few quiet minutes they departed, leaving him sole possession. His coffee came. He settled down comfortably with a copy of the local evening paper. But then, almost immediately, there came a tap at the door, and the manager appeared, bearing a bottle of Cognac.

'On the house, sir – for a distinguished guest.'

The manager himself had clearly been drinking. His hands shook as he put down the salver and poured out Cognac in two glasses. He handed one to Gently with an exaggerated flourish, then raised the other, slopping some of it.

'Your health, sir . . . if I may.'

Gently grunted and lifted his glass. The manager gulped down his own in one, as though it were a small drop of a considerable ocean. He eyed the bottle waterily.

'Your dinner, sir . . . satisfactory?'

'Quite satisfactory,' Gently said, putting down his tasted glass on the salver.

'Yes, sir . . . well . . . we have an excellent chef.' The manager made a vague little gesture with his glass. 'A first-class man . . . he came last year. That was before the takeover, of course.'

'I see,' Gently said. He rustled his paper.

'Yes, before the takeover,' the manager said. 'We were a Berney's house . . . though of course, you'll know that. I dare say . . . well, that's your business, isn't it?'

Gently looked at him. The manager winced slightly. He hovered swayingly, his thick lips parted. 'I mean, you consider everything . . . well, it stands to reason.' He licked his lips. 'There's my horse,' he said. 'I've got a horse . . . you know that?'

No,' Gently said. 'I didn't know that.'

'Well, I've got a horse,' the manager said, breathing heavily. He made the same little gesture with his glass, then picked up the bottle and slopped out more Cognac.

'More for you . . . ?'

Gently shook his head. The manager gulped some and looked round for a chair. He sat down suddenly, his knees close to Gently's, then stared for a while at his tremulous glass.

'Yes, a horse . . .

'What colour?' Gently said patiently.

'What . . . ? He's a bay, a light bay. Not that I keep him here, of course. He's over at Brunton, at a friend's farm. A five-year-old . . . thirteen hands. Over at Brunton, that's where he is.' He drank the rest of the glass. 'Used to come here,' he said.

'Who?'

'Who . . . ? Charlie Berney. Well . . . that stands to reason, doesn't it? I mean, in those days he owned the place . . .' The manager jerked his glass. 'Acted like it, too. Like he owned the place and everything in it. I could see you giving some of my customers a look . . . true enough. You weren't far out.'

'You didn't like him,' Gently said.

The manager wagged his head, sucking in air. 'Charlie Berney. But what could I do . . . ? He was the boss around here, wasn't he? So he comes in here . . . I hold my tongue. I mean, it's a good house, there's good money. In this business you have to stay in line . . . you can see that, can't you?'

Gently nodded. The manager reached for the bottle. Behind him, the door opened silently a few inches. Gently found himself staring at the smartly dressed woman whom he'd tagged as the manager's wife. She gazed at him unwaveringly for a moment, then silently closed the door again.

The manager drank.

'People don't realize . . . you don't know much about this business? You're never free . . . seven days a week . . . a couple of hours off if you're lucky. So what can you do . . . ? I mean if I neglected it . . . well, you can't. It's got to go on. So if people take advantage, if you can't trust them . . . well, you're caught. Can't you see?'

'Yes,' Gently said.

The manager drank. 'Oh, he had her,' he said. 'He bloody had her. All those times she wasn't at her mother's when I rang up . . . it stands to reason.' He trembled suddenly. 'And him still coming in . . . every evening, you understand? And me knowing, and him knowing I knew. The bastard. The bugger. Only what could I do . . . ?'

'What did you do?' Gently said.

The manager swayed his head, his stare glassy. Then his thick lips began to crumple.

'Bloody nothing,' he said.

★　★　★

105

Gently rose, went to the door, opened it and glanced into the passage; then he closed it again and returned to the manager, who sat kneading his glass between his palms.

'Let's get this clear,' Gently said. 'You're telling me you had reason for hating Berney. You've also told me you own a horse. All you need to show now is opportunity.'

'Opportunity . . . ?'

'What were you doing Tuesday?'

The manager scarcely seemed to take it in. 'Tuesday . . . I don't remember. Tuesday is sale-day. The farmers . . .'

'Was your wife here?'

'Rachel . . . ?' He licked his lips, but they stayed dry. 'I had to tell you . . . can't you see that? I knew you'd find out about the horse . . .'

'So what were you doing on Tuesday?'

'I was here . . . it's an extension . . .'

'Tuesday afternoon.'

'Yes . . . an extension. I can never get out on a Tuesday.' He swallowed the last little from his glass. 'I didn't do it,' he said. 'Don't think that. It was all over a year ago. But I know you wouldn't come here for nothing . . . not a man like you, straight to the William . . .'

Gently sighed to himself and sat again. For a moment a present seemed to have been dumped in his lap. But plainly the brandy-soaked man in front of him was just one more conscience-pricked Berney cuckold . . . provided like Drury with an asbestos alibi by Tuesday's having been a sale-day.

'And it was all over – a year ago.'

The manager gave some exaggerated nods. 'Rachel . . . well, I never had it out with her. But of course . . . I mean, it stands to reason.' He looked wretchedly at Gently. 'We don't sleep together. I've got a room across in the wing . . . ever since. It can't be the same . . . Christ knows how we'll finish up.'

'But Berney stopped coming here.'

'No, oh no. He was coming here after that, the bastard. He brought the Stogumber girl here . . . or she brought him, I don't know quite how it was. Then there was her brother, and the old man's cousin . . . they'd all come here in a party . . . Rachel, she wouldn't come down, but me of course . . . you see a hell of a lot, in this game.'

He paused to lick his lips again; his eyes rolled a little, then straightened.

'Tell you something . . . this is what I reckon. She'd given him a hoist with his own gear.'

Gently checked. 'How do you mean . . . ?'

The manager nodded his foolish nods. 'Take my word for it. She's got a bun . . . but who was the baker, I'd like to know? Not Charlie Berney . . . I'll swear to that! I mean, the way she treated him was a joke. And he couldn't see it, the stupid bugger . . . but I could see it, I tell you straight!'

Gently sat very still. 'She was deceiving him . . . ?'

The manager giggled knowingly and groped for the bottle. 'She was giving him a hoist . . . that's rich, isn't it? One bastard fathered on another, and him innocent as a babe . . .'

He poured more Cognac, chortling tipsily, with

moisture beading on his pickled nose. He drank. His swimming eyes tried to settle on Gently's, but kept missing them, going past them.

Gently got up and went out to the foyer, where there was a pay-telephone for customers. He fed in a coin and dialled the police station. A few seconds later he was connected to Docking.

'Listen,' Gently said. 'I've been talking to a genius, a man who can see the obvious when it's in front of him.' He wedged himself more firmly into the booth. 'Forget Berney's woman. Tomorrow, we'll be hunting for a man.'

CHAPTER NINE

THE OBVIOUS . . . ! And, after he'd slept on it, it remained no less obvious. With the morning sun slanting into his bedroom, Gently lay luxuriously checking over the points.

Now there was logic in that clapped-up marriage, in the mysterious behaviour of a playboy brewer, in the conspiracy of Lachlan Stogumber and the unwidowlike character of his sister . . .

Berney had been hoist. A middle aged Casanova, he'd been twisted round the finger of the haughty Marie. Dazzled by a sudden, miraculous complacence, he'd run his neck straight into the noose. And he'd been hoisted: the doughty warrior had become the gull of a young girl; learning too late that he'd been pre-cuckolded, was a mock-husband: a joke.

Gently stirred comfortably amongst the bedclothes. Starting from there, all the rest fitted! They had probably even a short-list of Berney's suspects, comprised by the names of those invited to his party. Because the party stood out as an evident ploy. It had been contrived to discover Marie's lover. Uncharacteristically subdued,

Berney had stayed in the background, waiting, watching for the unguarded exchange – which, it turned out, wasn't to come, since the contemptuous Marie had stuck close to her brother and Redmayne all evening. It was only later she'd made her slip: letting Berney get a glimpse of that damning sonnet.

Gently paused in his thoughts. What exactly had Berney seen? It didn't have to be the type copy which his wife had produced for the police. Once Mrs Berney realized that her domestic had talked, she could easily have provided herself with a duplicate from her brother's typewriter. But if there had been an original – say in manuscript, and signed – wouldn't Berney have known from that the identity of her lover? Which apparently he didn't, because the next day he'd set his trap to find it out. Gently frowned. Either the typescript was the original, or it was copied from one that was similarly anonymous . . .

One way or another – it had settled Berney! He certainly hadn't believed that the sonnet was her brother's. Sick with jealousy, he'd pretended a message calling him to London on business. To make the opportunity more inviting he'd invented a need to stay the night in town; then, after booking in at Starmouth, he'd gone straight to the heath to keep watch.

So far, so good: but here one came to the crux of the mystery. Why had Berney been so inflexibly confident that the rendezvous would be on the heath? He had made the opportunity himself, so there could have been no prior arrangement for him to be privy to, and if he didn't know the lover's identity and place of residence, he couldn't tell if the heath was convenient or not. Yet he appeared to have had no doubts. He had stationed himself unhesitatingly at the entry to the heath. And sure enough, his quarry had turned up, and he had followed her to the meeting-place . . .

Gently reached his pipe from the bedside cabinet, filled it and applied an absent match. As though – this was it! – Berney had guessed who his man was, and on Tuesday was seeking positive proof. He had guessed – and guessed rightly: the lover was going to come over the heath. He was a man who lived on the far side of the heath, who was familiar with the heath: and a riding man.

Gently closed his eyes and puffed. Before him he saw spread again Docking's map: the two red crosses – not so very far apart – and the heath ranging beyond, to Clayfield. Doubtless Marie had driven on to the heath and had concealed her car at the survey point. She couldn't drive fast on the rough track, so it was possible for Berney to follow her on foot. Or perhaps he'd hung back, knowing where she must park, and had watched her movements from far off – closing in then, by cutting across, when she began to head for the valley. However it was, she led him to the spot, and to that spot had come the horseman: across the heath. From some compass-bearing on the distant perimeter he'd ridden in . . .

From Clayfield?

Clayfield was farthest, but that didn't put it out of reckoning. Even on a hot day, at an easy pace, a horse could cover the distance in half an hour. And Rising had horses. He was acquainted with the Stogumbers. His wife, Jill, had taught Marie to ride. He was perhaps the sort of man Lachlan Stogumber might abet against the debauched brewer whom his sister had made use of. Stogumber might even have helped Rising with the sonnet, and typed it himself in case Berney did see it . . . that would square well with the young poet's character, and account for his confidence that Gently couldn't disprove his authorship. On the other counts, Rising had been at the party, and Rising had no checkable alibi . . .

Gently blew smoke at the slanted sunlight. Moving now to the other end of the heath! There – it stood out – was the Home Farm, in distance nearest to the place of the meeting. And there was the horse, the killer horse, already with a maimed groom to its record – unridable by anyone but Creke, by his own witness – though the man was almost certainly a liar. Not that Creke rated high as a suspect. One couldn't imagine him attracting Marie. His literary talent was probably zero, he hadn't been at the party, and his alibi was sound. It was the horse that didn't have an alibi, though Creke had done his best to provide it with one: the huge horse, with its satanic temper . . . ready to the hand of a man who dared.

And of course, there had been a man who'd dared.

Gently felt for the matches and relit his pipe. Occupying middle ground, between the Home Farm and Clayfield, the Manor House looked across the heath to the sea. A mile up the road from the stallion's stable. Say a couple of minutes in a bouncing Renault. A Renault, whose small, close wheels might have left narrow tracks under the trees by the stable . . .

Gently smiled to himself. It fitted almost too well – supposing his hypothesis was the right one. On every count, from alibi to literacy, Redmayne qualified as the hot suspect. It went further. He was an inmate with Marie before her hasty marriage to Berney – and, according to her brother, was exactly the type to whom Marie would feel attracted. Redmayne, as a poet, would probably be a traditionalist. Redmayne had access to Lachlan Stogumber's typewriter. Redmayne, beyond doubt, would get the poet's backing in any collision with the law. And to this one could add that Marie sought his company at the party, perhaps in defiance of her husband's gorgon gaze . . .

A hot suspect? Well . . . yes! But there was one tiny flaw in the argument. Gently impatiently struck another match and puffed rank smoke towards the ceiling. If Marie Stogumber had been pregnant by Redmayne, what was to stop her from marrying her lover? The affair with Berney would have been superfluous if Leo Redmayne had been the man. Possible to think up explanations, like Marie marrying Berney in a fit of pique . . . but probable? Gently shook his head. A fit of pique rarely led to such rashness.

He glanced at his watch. It showed five past eight. He pulled over the telephone that stood on the cabinet. When Docking came on he sounded brisk and mettle-some, as though he'd just stepped out of a cold shower.

'Don't wait for me,' Gently said. 'Carry on with checking the party guests. And remember, today we're not pulling punches – we need to get that list sorted.'

'Sir,' Docking said eagerly. 'I've been giving it some thought, sir, and there's one name on the list that really stands out.'

'Yes,' Gently said. 'But that one's for me.'

'Sir,' Docking said.

Gently hung up.

The manager didn't appear at breakfast, but his wife sat icily at their table by the wall. She had eyes for nobody, certainly not for Gently, and she rose and stalked out while he was still at his porridge.

In the foyer he met a couple of reporters, to whom he gave one of his famous pseudo-statements. Wistfully, they bowled him one or two fast ones, then let him go – knowing their Gently.

He fetched the Lotus and set out through the busy, Saturday-morning town. The sun was spiteful already, sitting lurid in a palish sky. A little thunderish? Towards the sea the horizon was dully clear and hard, while in the windscreen buzzed another black fly such as Docking had executed the day before. Some weather breeding . . .

Coming to the Home Farm, Gently eased the Lotus to a crawl. Creke had cleared his barley. The field by the track lay shaven and empty except for scattered straw-bales. A long way off, on a gentle slope, the orange-painted combine was still chuntering restlessly, but here, where the stable stood shadowy in its dark trees, nothing stirred, no man came. Gently hunched and drove on. This was the way it had been on Tuesday! For a man whose convenience it was to use him the black stallion had waited. For a man who could ride him . . .

The Manor House lay silent in the steep sun, its door and most of its windows wide open. Gently drifted the Lotus through the yews and let it glide to a halt by the

114

brick steps. A movement caught his eye, in the trees to the right. He recognized Redmayne stooping over some object. At the same moment Redmayne caught sight of him, straightened, remained for a second motionless. Then he came slowly forward, carrying something in his hand.

'Look ... *Panolis griseovarigata*. There's a brood making hay of that young *Pinus*.'

He opened his hand to reveal a small, lively caterpillar, with linear stripes of green, white and orange.

Gently stared at it. 'Is it something rare?'

'A typical layman's remark,' Redmayne grinned. 'No, there's nothing rare about this – it's only too common for some arboriculturalists.' He turned his hand over, letting the caterpillar climb it, and following its movements with smiling eyes. 'It's death to pine trees,' he said. 'But what a lovely creature. And the moth too. It's the Pine Beauty.'

'Thanks,' Gently said. 'I'll remember that.'

Redmayne laughed and settled the caterpillar on a leaf. 'So you haven't called in to naturalize,' he said. 'More's the pity. Who do you want?'

'I want you.'

'Do you?' Redmayne said. 'Well, I'm probably the most conversible. But I was planning a little ramble on the heath. I suppose we couldn't combine our activities?'

Gently hesitated. 'Very well,' he said.

Redmayne grinned. 'You won't regret it. Just give me a minute to go into the house, and then we'll be on our way.'

He ran up the steps. Gently leaned against the Lotus

and began to fill his pipe. All about the Manor was quiet, except for the crooning of wood-pigeons in one of the beeches. A remote place ... According to Docking's map, there was nothing nearer to the Manor than the Home Farm, and that was a mile distant. Just the fields, the woods and the heath ...

He heard steps in the hall and turned, but it was Lachlan Stogumber who'd come to the door. He stood staring contemptuously at Gently and Lotus, his large, goldeny eyes inimical.

'We'll have to find you a room, officer,' he said. 'What's the latest – has the horse confessed?'

Gently regarded the young man mildly. He was dressed this morning in a white, Shelleyan shirt, its front unbuttoned to the waist.

'Perhaps I've dreamed up a new mystery woman,' Gently said.

Lachlan Stogumber laughed jeeringly. 'You'll have to do better than dream,' he said. 'Jill Rising wasn't a very bright guess.'

'Perhaps now I'm a little closer than Mrs Rising.'

'But not close enough. You'll never be that.'

'Perhaps almost as close as I am now to you.'

Lachlan Stogumber paused, his eyes staring fiercely.

'Yesterday,' Gently said, 'I was looking at it one way. Today, I'm looking at it in another. And today it's fitting a great deal better. We probably won't need a confession from the horse.'

'What are you insinuating—?'

Lachlan Stogumber stepped forward, anger thinning his handsome face. But just then Redmayne reappeared to lay a hasty hand on the poet's arm.

116

'Manners, Lally,' he smiled. 'Don't give the Super the wrong impression.'

Lachlan Stogumber jerked his arm away and flashed his cousin a furious glare. For a spell they stood confronting each other, Redmayne calm, Lachlan Stogumber smouldering; then the latter broke away and marched offendedly into the house. Redmayne gave a faint shrug.

'Poets . . . ! But somebody has to live with the breed.' He came down the steps. 'But never mind Lally. There's a *Cuscuta europaea* I'm going to show you.'

Redmayne's friendliness was difficult to ignore, and he had a gift for transmitting his enthusiasm. Falling into step beside Gently, he was soon chatting unconcernedly about *C. europaea* and *C. epithymum*. He was wearing the same gear as yesterday, the khaki bush-shirt and drab trousers, with binoculars and collecting-case slung on either side and a broad-brimmed linen hat on his head. A bachelor of fifty: a contented man. You could scarcely imagine him at odds with life. Almost certainly, in his background would be a comfortable competence, safely invested.

He marshalled Gently back down the yew-alley and across the road, into the rough pasture. Here a footpath led to a stile, and over the stile they were on the heath. At this point a number of stony ridges spread out before them like the fingers of a hand, but Redmayne unhesitatingly chose his track and brought them, with a stiff scramble, on to the plateau. Here he paused to survey the wide prospect. Some two miles of heath stretched between them and the village. A broken, undulating plain, brushed with the throbbing blue of heather, it gave an impression of darkness, of sombreness, even under the staring sun.

Redmayne pointed to the haze, now well established on the far skyline.

'It's now or never for old Creke. He won't be cutting at this time tomorrow.'

'Is he nearly finished?' Gently asked.

'Haven't seen him to ask,' Redmayne said. 'But he'll soon be round if the rain catches him out – he's always nagging about his rent.'

He set off at an easy pace, heading roughly towards the village. For a while he walked in silence, a half-smile on his lips. Then he turned to Gently.

'Come on,' he said. 'The Great Man has been doing some thinking. I overheard your conversation with Lachlan, and I'm not so dumb that I missed the drift of it.'

Gently shrugged. 'Then you'll know what I'm after.'

'Pretty well,' Redmayne agreed. 'But it doesn't follow that I can help you.'

'Would you if you could?'

Redmayne spread his hands.

They tramped on a little farther.

'You know, you've got problems,' Redmayne said, smiling. 'As you may have noticed, we're a little world on our own. High Hale Manor is Stogumber Castle. A self-contained world – perhaps too much so for everybody's good. It produces certain attitudes, certain characters. And that's been going on for centuries.'

Gently let two paces go. 'Are we talking of Lachlan?'

Redmayne nodded. 'Both he and Marie. A pair of nestlings of the Manor House, brought up without maternal supervision. Oh, I'm sure Jimmy did his best with them, and there's always been our excellent Lottie. But the end result is a couple of young hawks who scorn to fly at a common pitch. Lachlan – well, he's the Wonderful Boy, with talent enough for half a dozen. And Marie's not a feather behind him. All the rest of the world are choughs and daws.' He paused. 'And that's your problem. They'd never tell tales on one another. What Lachlan knows about Marie's secrets is too fine for peasants like you and I.'

Gently grunted. 'But you're resident at the Manor.'

'Yes, I grant you that,' Redmayne smiled.

'And not entirely above eavesdropping,' Gently said.

'That's naughty,' Redmayne grinned. 'And not wholly justified.'

He halted suddenly, staying Gently with his hand, and slewed the binoculars to his eyes. About fifty yards off a small bird had flitted from one patch of gorse to the next. Redmayne watched it intently for some moments; then clicked his tongue and lowered the binoculars.

'*P. domesticus*,' he said. 'Life is full of disappointments. I'm keeping my eyes skinned for Dartford Warblers – improbable, but this place is full of surprises.'

They resumed their walking, descending now into a shallow, gorsy depression. Redmayne sniffed appreciatively at the heady scent that seemed a live presence in the hot, still air.

'You see – what you want to know isn't so simple, even for an eavesdropping resident like me. Our two aristos are so darned choosy about the company they keep. That goes with the sex thing too. I told you Lachlan wasn't greatly interested. Well, it's much the same with Marie. She's highly inclined to bite a fellow's head off.'

'Nevertheless, she's beautiful,' Gently said.

'Oh yes, they buzz round her,' Redmayne agreed. 'And Marie's not averse to a bit of attention, provided the mujiks know their place. But she's never to my knowledge had a regular beau, or put herself out for any male whatever. I imagine the only reason she tolerated Charles was because he was prepared to go around on his knees.'

Gently nodded. 'So the young men didn't interest her.'

'That's what I'm saying,' Redmayne said.

'And you wouldn't know why.'

Redmayne looked at him quickly. 'Only the reason I've given you,' he said.

'Couldn't she have been already suited?'

Redmayne was silent. The expression in his eyes was curious.

'Say, by a rather older man,' Gently continued. 'A man given to writing traditional love-sonnets?'

For a fraction of a second Redmayne's eyes jerked wider, then they softened, and he started to laugh. From one of the buttoned pockets in his bush shirt he produced a small paperback with an orange jacket.

'I guessed which way you were thinking,' he said, 'when you grabbed me just now. So I thought I'd fetch this along: here you are – Leo Redmayne, poet!'

★ ★ ★

Gently took the paperback. It was a little rubbed, and the style of the jacket not contemporary. It was, in fact, a Fougasse design, dating back to the immediate post-war period. It exhibited a fig with oriental features that grinned toothily at the beholder, and was titled, in the pseudo-casual Fougasse script: *Chinese Figs/Leo Raymond*. Gently flicked it open. Each page contained a single quatrain and an illustration. On page i the jacket illustration re-appeared, and beneath it Gently read:

Consider now the Chinese Fig,
　　Which, if not little, must be big;
　Or, being large, cannot be small –
　Or else there is no fig at all!

'That's the great original,' Redmayne smiled. 'The first veritable Chinese Fig. I knocked those together while I was waiting to be demobbed – it's my most popular publication. They reprint it every other Christmas.'

Gently grunted and thumbed over the pages. Each verse was a comparable nonsense doggerel. They ranged from a dolphin who went golfin to scientists in shipses recording absurd eclipses. Silently, Gently handed the book back.

'A far call from love sonnets?' Redmayne suggested.

Gently said nothing.

'At least,' Redmayne said, 'you must admit that sonnets are more Lally's line than mine. And he's quite serious about this change of direction. Lally regards himself as the first pre-Tennysonite. Eliot and non-poetry are suddenly *passé* – soon, not a student will be seen dead with it. If Lally claims the sonnet, then he'll have written it.'

'That's not what Berney thought,' Gently said.

Redmayne gestured. 'Charlie was jealous. Also, the fact of the sonnet being in traditional form would throw him, just as it's now throwing you. All Charlie knew about was Lally's other stuff, which he couldn't make head or tail of.' He hesitated. 'The sonnet was typed, was it – didn't have any identification?'

Gently shrugged. 'It was typed – on Lachlan Stogumber's typewriter.'

'That's it, then – Charlie wouldn't recognize it. He thought it came from some Romeo, and blew his top.'

Gently stared at him. 'Does your cousin lock up his typewriter?'

'Oh, oh!' Redmayne grinned. 'That's below the belt. He doesn't lock it up, but the study belongs to him, and using the typewriter would constitute a lèse-majesté.'

'But Marie could have used it. Or someone else.'

'To put it delicately,' Redmayne smiled.

'Someone who might have been planning a face-saver – in case the sonnet did come to Berney's notice.'

Redmayne tucked away the paperback, shaking his head.

'You know why Marie Stogumber married Berney,' Gently said. 'She was three months pregnant and looking for a scapegoat. In the normal way she wouldn't have looked at Berney.'

Redmayne hunched a shoulder. 'Couldn't Berney have been the father?'

'It wasn't Berney who wrote the sonnet.'

'Nor, I assure you, was it me.'

122

'But you could be a liar,' Gently said. 'Couldn't you?'

Redmayne only smiled. He slid an amused glance at Gently. 'That's not a serious accusation,' he said. 'You and I are two people who rather like each other. I might fib to you, but I couldn't deceive you.'

'One way or the other, you know who the man is.'

Redmayne nodded. 'I can't stop you thinking it. But even if I did – and I don't concede that – you'll understand that I must protect Marie. What would you think of me if I didn't?'

'I might think you value your liberty,' Gently said.

Redmayne laughed and laid a hand on his elbow. 'Come along,' he said. 'Light in our darkness. Another hundred yards, and we'll see the *europaea*.'

At the lowest part of the depression was a clump of scrub thorn and a single, ancient, elder-bush that bore a few clusters of green berries. Near the elder protruded a few flints, bound together with mouldering plaster.

'*Et voilà!*' Redmayne pointed to some nettles. One or two of their stiff stalks were encircled with reddish cords. Small bundles of white flowers, which appeared at first to belong to the nettles, on closer examination were seen to sprout from the parasitic stems.

Gently gazed at them, and then at Redmayne. 'Is this what we've crossed the heath to look at?'

'O barbarian!' Redmayne exclaimed. 'You are present at a botanical event. This is the first time *C. europaea* has been certainly recorded in the county. For this if no other you'll find my name in the great scroll.'

'Has it a common name?'

Redmayne nodded. 'The vulgar call it Greater Dodder.'

'And it is truly rare?'

'Truly. The next nearest is probably in Kent.'

'Yet you found it,' Gently said. 'These few strands, on all the heath. I think you must spend a lot of your time here. I think perhaps you're here almost every day.'

Redmayne nodded again. 'And so?' he said.

'This is where Mrs Berney met her lover. And he wouldn't be so hard to spot as *C. europaea*. So if you didn't see him, why didn't you?'

Redmayne gave his slight little shrug. He moved nearer to the nettles, stooped, and fingered one of the flower-heads. There was a great gentleness in the way he touched it, lifting and displaying the crisp inflorescence.

'You won't give up easily, will you?' he said. 'And that's what we laymen never allow for. The way you continue to put on pressure when any reasonable man would throw in his hand. We've got the answers, that's what we think, and you should accept them and go away.' He smiled sadly at Gently. 'But you don't go away. You just make the answers sound sillier and sillier.'

'But facts do stay facts,' Gently said.

'Yes, but there are different viewpoints,' Redmayne said. '*C. europaea* is a fact, both to you and to me, yet how very disparate is our experience of the fact. To me, it's near-poetry, a revelation, more memorable than the heather or the scent of the gorse. To you, it's an insignificant appendage of a nettle. But we're both looking at the same thing.'

'Only,' Gently said, 'my viewpoint is defined for me. Any latitude is left for the courts.'

'Yet it could still be a wrong one,' Redmayne smiled. 'Or proceeding with definitions too narrow to comprehend the full fact.'

He gave the flower-head a last, affectionate caress, then motioned with his hand in the direction of the village. They set off again through the sullen heat, which remained untempered by the growing haze.

'Let me take an example,' Redmayne said. 'Do you believe in accident-proneness?'

'Underwriters do,' Gently shrugged. 'And I've met a few people they wouldn't insure.'

'Just so,' Redmayne said. 'And have you noticed how it seems to be infectious? It isn't only the person involved who is prone to accidents, but he seems to share the proneness with the people around him.'

'Well?' Gently grunted.

Redmayne took a few strides. 'I think it's the same with tragedy,' he said. 'In my experience there are tragedy-prone people. And in that category I'd put the Stogumbers.'

Gently threw him a stare. 'You mean the curse?'

'Oh, don't under-rate curses,' Redmayne smiled. 'A curse may very well exist as a state of mind that predisposes its victim towards his fate. I'd rank the Stogumber curse as something like that. It's been dogging the family since the seventeenth century. And remember, Marie was brought up with the curse, which gives you the choice only of a sad life or a bad end.'

'And you're saying she passed it on to Berney?' Gently said.

Redmayne shook his head. 'Not quite like that. My theory is that Marie is a tragedy-prone person, with the power to give a tragic inflection to events.' He turned earnestly to Gently. 'Look detachedly at what's happened. It shouldn't have been tragedy – it should have been farce. Charlie, the old lecher, marrying a young girl, and finding out too late that she had a lover. That's farce – and so was the rest of it, Charlie behaving like an ass to unmask his rival. But then, somehow, the wrong chance came up – the millionth chance – and the farce was tragedy.'

'And it was Marie who brought up the millionth chance . . . ?'

'I don't know how else one can explain it. In the powerful emotional pressures of the situation, her tragic influence became energized. Suppose there was a stray on the heath – suppose, if you like, it was Nat's stallion. Is it impossible to accept that Marie's influence attracted it, even roused it to a fury against Charlie? Reaction to human emotion by animals is a fact, and the horse has always been regarded as a psychic beast.'

He looked keenly at Gently. Gently said nothing.

'Perhaps you think I'm talking nonsense,' Redmayne said. 'But I mean it seriously – and I'm kin to the Stogumbers. I'm only too convinced it could have happened like that.'

Gently's shoulders twitched. 'I would need a witness.'

'You'd hardly expect Marie or the fellow to confess.'

'Even though it were an accident?'

'Even so. Their going through the mangle wouldn't bring back Charlie.'

'It would make me go away.'

Redmayne looked rueful. 'And is it the only thing that would?'

Gently didn't say anything. Redmayne sighed.

They tramped on together, keeping step.

CHAPTER TEN

R ATHER MORE THAN half-way across the heath, Redmayne called a halt at the top of a ridge. The haze had now climbed up to the sun, which smouldered whitely behind it, like a pulsing wheel. Below it, seaward, a dark, blind curtain was shutting across the dimmed skyline, and hot, waspish little gusts were driving over the heath, spinning bents and leaf-rubbish as they came.

Redmayne grimaced at Gently. 'Time to get off or get wet,' he said. 'I was going to show you an *Oboranche eliator, anglice* Tall Broomrape, but it would have been past its best anyway.'

'Which is the nearest,' Gently asked, 'the Manor or the village?'

'The village,' Redmayne said, 'but there isn't much in it.'

'I think I'll continue to the village.'

Redmayne slowly nodded. 'I thought you would.'

He eased his broad-brimmed hat and resettled it, his hazel eyes mildly reproachful. 'I suppose it's no use reasoning with you,' he said. 'You'll go your policeman's way regardless.'

Gently shrugged. 'That's why you pay me.'

'But you're human too,' Redmayne said. 'This is a wretched business, and you can't make it better. Shouldn't you hesitate before making it worse?'

Gently was silent. Redmayne fingered the hat, pushed it up off his brow again.

'Well,' he said at last, 'go easy with her. You may think she's to blame, but she has a heart.'

'Are you coming with me?' Gently asked.

Redmayne shook his head. 'You'll find me at the Manor. By now, I imagine, you and I misunderstand each other about as well as we're ever likely to.' He grinned wryly. 'Keep to the ridges. They'll take you across to the survey point. And don't hang about – it isn't pleasant to be caught out here in a real pelter.'

He pulled down his hat, turned quickly and strode briskly away in the direction of the Manor. In a few moments his tall figure dipped below the ridge-top and disappeared.

Gently kept to the ridges. Another quarter of an hour's walking brought the edge of the plateau into view, and he was surprised suddenly to recognize below him the spot where Berney's body had been found. Automatically, he checked his watch. It was nearly an hour and a half since he'd left the Manor. Deducting time for the detour to view the *C. europaea*, the spot was approximately an hour's walk from the Manor. And coming the other way . . . ? He glanced towards the survey point. Twenty minutes at the outside, allowing five for the circumstance of the lady's being *enceinte* . . .

He frowned down at the narrow valley. It really was

an anonymous sort of place! Until the thicket of hawthorn had registered with him, he'd taken it for just one more of the heath's multitudinous folds. From the survey point it wouldn't be easy to find, and from the heath behind many times more difficult. From Clayfield, for example, it would almost be easier to head from the survey point, and to start from there . . .

Yet, on the other hand, for an illicit meeting, the spot could scarcely have been bettered. Lost entirely in the empty heath, it might have kept a secret for ever. Berney, guessing the heath, hadn't been able to guess farther, though presumably the heath wasn't strange to him. A perfect spot . . . but needing a man who knew the heath like his own face.

A gust of chiller wind puffed along the ridge, and soundless lightning lit the wrack seaward. Gently shivered and set off once more, aiming for the track below the survey point. The blue of the heather had gone dull and the bright scatters of gorse had faded. The sombre swartness that underlay the heath seemed suddenly to surface, like an alerted animal. He reached the track. Then he heard a low moaning of the wind, hollow and eerie.

Ten minutes later, when he got to the road, the first fat drops were splashing in the dust.

By the time he reached the Lodge it was raining busily, and he was sodden at the knees and shoulders. Haynes, the domestic, answered his ring, and stood staring at him disapprovingly before letting him in.

'Mrs Berney is upstairs. If you'll just wait . . .'

She left him in the hall while she went on her errand.

The house was silent: the buzz of rain outside sounded remote, in a separate world.

Mrs Berney appeared on the landing to gaze malevolently down at Gently. She was wearing a smock dress which concealed her bump yet gave no hint of being designed for maternity. She swung down the stairs with springy grace.

'Something I can do for you?' she asked insolently. 'If we're no longer issuing our policemen with raincoats, I may be able to find you an old one of Charlie's.'

'Thank you,' Gently said gravely. 'I may accept that.'

'Oh, I'm sure you would,' Mrs Berney said. 'And probably a bowl of soup if I had one, but I'm afraid the soup's gone for swill. What do you want?'

'Just some information.'

'Then why not try the public library.'

'I don't think it would have it,' Gently smiled. 'At least, it won't have it yet.'

Her grey eyes flashed at him with a ferocity that was reminiscent of her brother's. 'I know what you're after,' she said. 'Lachlan rang me. So don't waste your time smarming me.'

'Shall we talk, then?'

'It won't do you any good. But then, of course, it might amuse me.'

'So,' Gently said. 'You've nothing to lose.'

'Only my temper with policemen,' Mrs Berney said.

She gazed spite at him for another moment, then tossed her hair and crossed to the lounge. Gently followed. She stalked through the room and dropped into a high, throne-like Hepplewhite chair. Gently closed the door. Notwithstanding its bays, the lounge was gloomy in the dulled light; and perhaps because of them the rain sounded louder, a hissing beat on the gravel outside. Gently chose an easy chair and sat. A little thunder was crumpling softly, directly overhead.

'Do you believe in witchcraft, policeman?' Mrs Berney said.

'I believe in punishing it,' Gently said.

Mrs Berney laughed jeeringly. 'A proper policeman's answer! But you may believe in it yet, before you've finished here. And you wouldn't be able to burn me, you know. I have the classic plea in my tummy. So I could raise the devil from that rug in front of you, and not a single thing you could do about it.' She laughed again.

'Are you a witch?' Gently said.

'Perhaps,' Mrs Berney said. 'At least, I have a demon lover, which is the part that interests you. But like all demon lovers mine is invisible, he comes to me in a cloud of night. Perhaps I dream him. Do you think that's possible? The way Endymion dreamed of Artemis?'

Gently shook his head. 'Your lover is human enough.'

'Of course, he comes in human form.' Mrs Berney said. 'That's understood. He couldn't make love if he were merely incarnate spirit. But which human form – that's the question, isn't it? For all you know, he changes it nightly. I'm positive that's what Charlie thought. He suspected everyone who wore trousers.'

The room expanded briefly in a gleam of lightning. Mrs Berney sat shadowed in the sudden light. At the end of a stretched interval the thunder rippled subduedly, sounding very lofty above the house.

'Why did you marry Berney?' Gently asked.

'For the reason you find so obvious,' Mrs Berney said.

'Is it obvious?'

She sat motionless in her darkness, erect and tall in the straight-backed chair.

'We're living in permissive times,' Gently said. 'Not much stigma attaches to unmarried mothers. You are not poor. There is no economic reason why you could not have had your child at home. Alternatively, abortion is now legal, and you have the means to make it easily possible. Yet you don't choose either of these ways. You marry Berney. Why?'

Her laughter was biting. 'Because I chose to. Who are you to ask me for reasons?'

'Were you afraid of your father?'

'I'm afraid of nobody.'

'Your brother?'

Her laughter pealed through the room. 'My lover is a demon,' she said. 'Let that be your answer. I have a demon's child in my belly. Demons don't like their children to be bastards, nor do they permit them to be got rid of. And furthermore I want to have my child.' She gave a breathless chuckle. 'Aren't you curious to know what it will be?'

'You must have hated Berney,' Gently said.

'Why should I bother to hate such a creature?'

'Because you were his prisoner.'

'I a prisoner!' Her silky mane flicked across her shoulders. 'He was the prisoner. I laid a spell on him. Charlie was bound hand and foot. He was locked up in the cell of his jealousy. He knew I was loved, but he could never catch the lover. Oh, he was the prisoner, make no mistake – he married a witch, the poor fool.'

133

'But he would still be a threat.'

'No threat to me.'

'He had the rights of a husband.'

'Never,' she said. 'Do you suppose I would have let him sleep with me, when I was fresh from the arms of my lover?'

'But surely . . . to begin with?'

She shook her head forcefully. 'I told him on the wedding-night,' she said. 'It took the poor fool an hour to understand it, and then he reacted like any other peasant.'

'How did he react?'

'He brandished a penknife. He threatened to kill me unless I told him the name.'

'And then?'

Mrs Berney laughed mockingly. 'He came to heel. Like any other peasant.'

The thunder growled suddenly, now sounding much closer, then lightning glowed, and the thunder came again. Mrs Berney raised her hand.

'Perhaps he's up there now,' she said. 'My lover. Aren't you just a little afraid?'

Gently hunched a shoulder. 'So he came to heel,' he said. 'You told him his role, and he agreed to play it.'

'What else could he do?' she said. 'He was besotted with me. I probably stole his nail-parings and gave him philtres.'

'He didn't ever rebel.'

'He was too bemused. No doubt he thought that one day I'd come round. I was a sort of woman he'd never dealt with before, he didn't know what was making me tick.'

'But he'd watch you.'

'Oh yes.'

'Wouldn't that make things difficult?'

'Not for me,' she laughed. 'My lover walks by night. Charlie watched and watched, but discovered nothing.'

'Not at the party?'

'Not then. The poem was Lachlan's, and Charlie had to accept it.'

'But he didn't accept it,' Gently said. 'He set a trap for you.'

'And it was he who fell in it,' Mrs Berney said.

The lightning flared, to be followed by a sharp detonation of thunder. Mrs Berney jumped up, then, checking herself, moved calmly to one of the bays and stared out at the rain. It was whirring down fast now. Straight, steady rods of it rumbled on the gravel and bowed the leaves of the rhododendrons. Over the lawn, still fawn-patched with drought, it raised a fine mist of bouncing spray.

'Of course, you can never marry him,' Gently said.

'Who cares about marriage,' she said. 'I've tried it.'

'There can't be any future. We shall keep watch on you. When he comes to you, we shall have the murderer.'

She laughed softly. 'It's funny,' she said. 'But now you're reminding me of Charlie. Once I had a jealous husband on the watch for my lover, now I have a jealous policeman. And what makes you think you'll do better than Charlie? He was living with me, day by day. He kept a watch on my bedroom at night. And it was no use – love found a way.'

'But, at last, he did spot his man,' Gently said.

'No, never,' she said. 'He was still guessing. He was guessing when he set his puerile trap, and went out on the heath, and the stallion trampled him.'

'So it was Creke's stallion,' Gently said. 'Thank you.'

Mrs Berney turned from the window haughtily. 'That's scarcely worthy of you,' she said. 'It was you who said it was the stallion. Another peurile trap. But you are wasting your time – you'll never know what happened out there. This is far away, outside your knowledge, beyond the wit of Scotland Yard.'

'You could try me,' Gently said.

She tossed her head. 'You are still in the outer darkness. How can you understand our enlightenment, the sudden step forward into freedom? My lover is a king, a god. Without such a love you must remain in ignorance. We laugh at the slave world of the mortals where contingency rules and no freedom is possible.'

Gently shrugged. 'I've come across such illusions. They're usually connected with L.S.D.'

'Acid.' She laughed. 'I've tried acid. But acid is passé, my poor friend. Mere chemical joys are for the slaves. Opium is the religion of the masses. But we're beyond that, beyond the slave-tricks. Don't bother searching the house for drugs.'

Lightning bleached the room and left fizzing gloom, and thunder hammered the roofs again. Mrs Berney stood with raised hands, as though claiming the pounding uproar for her own. She let her hands fall. She moved closer to Gently.

'You should have a little fear,' she said. 'A mortal man,

dealing with things immortal. With a demon who rides such a storm as this.'

'Not to mention Creke's stallion,' Gently said.

'Would he need to ride it?' she said. 'He could reach from the moon to lift the stable-latch, and send the stallion out on the heath. What other than that will you learn?'

'A name. To go with yours on the charge sheet.'

Her laugh was shrill. 'But if he has no name?'

'Then perhaps yours will stand there alone.'

Her hand swept up as though to strike him, its long fingers outspread: then she checked, staring past Gently. The lights had come on. Lachlan Stogumber had entered.

'Easy,' he said. 'Easy, sister. Don't let this gentleman get you stirred up.'

He closed the door and came into the room, his gaze fixed tightly on his sister.

'But Lally, he's accusing me—'

'I heard. But losing your head won't do any good. And of course, it's a try-on, he doesn't know anything. So cool down, stop playing his game.'

He stood close to her, forceful and intent, staring down her wild indignation. For some moments she resisted him, her eyes hating; but she bit her lip and kept silent. Lachlan Stogumber turned to Gently.

'You're an expert,' he said, 'aren't you? Getting people to flip is your big thing. Perhaps it's as well I came when I did.'

Gently hunched. 'Why did you come?'

'Because I ran into Leo,' Lachlan Stogumber said. 'He

was going to drive round and pick you up himself, but I decided to save him the trip. Also, I thought Marie might need a little support.'

'Very brotherly of you,' Gently said.

Lachlan Stogumber shook his head. 'Oh no,' he said. 'I've learned my lesson. Don't waste your talent.' He turned back to his sister. 'Has he upset you?' he said.

Mrs Berney tossed her hair sulkily. 'The man's a fool,' she said. 'He thinks he can understand me. That's the only reason why I'm upset, Lally.'

Lachlan Stogumber grinned. 'No cause to worry, then.'

'He thinks I knew about the stallion.'

'And did you?'

She flashed angry eyes at him. 'Only that you told me he was asking about it.'

'So I did,' Lachlan Stogumber said, smiling. 'And that's the perfect answer, Marie. And as for him understanding you, you're quite right. Any man who thinks he can do that is a fool.'

Her angry stare lasted another moment, then slowly it softened into a smile.

'Take him away,' she said. 'I'm tired of the fellow. Let him have another go at you and Leo.'

'Leo he's done. Leo's very thoughtful.'

Mrs Berney's smile faded. 'Well anyway, get him off my back. I feel insulted all the time he's here.'

They stayed looking at each other. The thunder rumbled outside. The lights in the room dipped and brightened. Lachlan Stogumber shrugged his neat shoulders and glanced at Gently: Gently rose.

CHAPTER ELEVEN

T HE STORM WAS moving inland. As Lachlan
Stogumber eased his TR4 down the Lodge drive,
Gently, seated beside him, could see the blackest of the
wrack lying heavy and low over the heath. The heath
itself was dark as pitch, its long cliff-line vague at the
edges; silvery veins and bursts of lightning momentarily
sharpened it, etching detail. Then the thunder crashed.
The rain, unabated, was getting the better of the
Triumph's wipers. Along with them down the drive
gushed a small torrent, and a stream was rilling across the
village street.

Lachlan Stogumber drove cautiously and with a
smoothness that Gently appreciated. He hadn't said
anything since they'd dived through the rain to feed
themselves quickly into the Triumph's cramped quar-
ters. His hands light on the wheel, he stared intently
ahead, his attention apparently all on the driving. They
hissed steadily through the deserted village, made the
turn right for Low Hale.

At the entry to the heath, Lachlan Stogumber slowed.
'Is this a good place for a talk?' he said.

Gently was silent. Lachlan Stogumber turned off, drove some yards up the track, parked and switched off. He sat still, looking out at the drenched heath. The rain boomed on the car and flooded down the windscreen. Hatchings of lightning seemed to split sideways, pouring sudden, sick radiance across the black acres.

'An omen too late,' Lachlan Stogumber said. 'We should have had this storm on Tuesday. But I doubt whether the gods would have bothered about Charlie – they didn't open the graves to portend the deaths of brewers.'

'It could still be an omen,' Gently said. 'And not too late.'

'Dear me, you're superstitious,' Lachlan Stogumber said. 'I thought all that was left to poets these days. And women, naturally. Logic hasn't made them fools.' He lit a cigarette, filling the small car with smoke. 'You think I can name him for you, don't you?' he said. 'You were marvellously slow getting off the mark with Marie, but now you have the feeling you're home and dry.' He grinned. 'Right?' he said.

Gently nodded. 'You know,' he said.

'I know,' Lachlan Stogumber said. 'I'm in Marie's confidence. The world else may not know, but me you can rely on. And yet' – he inhaled smoke – 'suppose I don't know. Suppose, after all, you're up the wrong tree again. Suppose Marie doesn't, never did have a lover, and that the child she is carrying is all Charlie's?'

Gently stared out at the darkness. 'It's no use. I've spoken to her.'

'Yes, but you don't know Marie,' Lachlan Stogumber said. 'Marie's a romantic, a Walter Mitty character.

She'll accept any role you offer her, if it's suitably dramatic. And I tipped her off. She knew what you wanted. She was all set to play it for you when you arrived. And if I know my sister she laid it on thick, especially with a thunderstorm going for her. Isn't that what happened?'

Gently's shoulders twitched.

'You see, I do know her,' Lachlan Stogumber said. 'And the fact of the matter is she's never had a lover. If the child isn't Charlie's, it doesn't make sense.'

'Does anything different make sense?' Gently asked.

Lachlan Stogumber trailed smoke. 'Not with murder in mind. But don't you see, murder only came into it because of Charlie's reputation as a debauchee. Apart from that, his death was an accident – one unusual, but not unknown – and if you allow that jealousy was the cause of his behaviour, then you come back to accident. No actual lover is necessary.'

'And the writer of the sonnet . . . ?'

'Myself, of course. Some day you're going to have to believe that.'

Gently shook his head. 'That's where it falls down. I don't believe it, and I'm not likely to.'

Lachlan Stogumber sighed. 'A pity,' he said. 'I've tried to treat you like an intelligent man. But I'll make one more effort. You wanted to see my original manuscript, and I've brought it for you. Here.'

He felt in his breast pocket and brought out a notebook from which he took a crumpled, torn-out leaf. He gave the leaf to Gently. It bore a copy of the sonnet written in a small, nervous hand. Here and there a differing word or phrase had been struck out and one or more alternatives written above it. It added up to the text which Gently had and was dated with Monday's date.

'This is your handwriting?'

For answer Lachlan Stogumber took out his pen. He took the sheet from Gently, smoothed it on the notebook, and signed his name. The writing was identical.

'Good enough?'

Gently shook his head again. 'You could easily have manufactured this.'

Lachlan Stogumber laughed ironically. 'I put the truth in your hands, and still you ask for proof and more proof. Well, proof you shall have.' He flicked through the note-book and carefully detached another leaf from it. 'Here's something you haven't seen, didn't know about, couldn't have guessed at. A second sonnet.'

He thrust the leaf at Gently. Gently stared at him, then at the leaf. In Stogumber's handwriting, with crossings and corrections, was inscribed another sonnet in the style of the first.

'Read it,' Lachlan Stogumber commanded.

'Why should I bother?' Gently shrugged. 'The one is no more proof than the other. They are merely two samples of your handwriting.'

'They are mine. My poems.'

'So you tell me.'

'There is nobody else who could have written them.'

'Just one poet – for the Stogumber poetry.'

Lachlan Stogumber's eyes blazed. 'What do you mean?'

Gently placed the two leaves in his wallet. 'I would

have thought it was simple logic,' he said. 'Somebody in High Hale is a poet, but that somebody isn't Mrs Berney's brother. So who is he? Who writes the poetry? If it's one and the same person, it isn't you. And if it isn't one and the same person, you didn't write the sonnets. Which way do you want it to be?'

Lachlan Stogumber's expression was murderous. 'It is I – only I – who write my poetry!'

'Yet you're trying to take credit for someone else's poems.'

'They're mine, all of them. All mine!'

Gently shrugged. Lachlan Stogumber sat glaring, his mouth dragged in a thin line. The rain kept pounding. Little thin nets of lightning flickered afar off, moving inland. Lachlan Stogumber stabbed out his cigarette.

'My God, you say dangerous things,' he said. 'No wonder Marie wanted to strike you. But that's policemen the world over – peasants, trying to reduce you to their own level.'

'Trying to find the truth,' Gently said. 'From people whose levels have sunk too low.'

'Peasants,' Lachlan Stogumber said. 'Sadistic peasants. Dressed in authority and hypocritical sentiments. And the truth I told you.'

'No,' Gently said. 'Not the truth. I want a name.'

Lachlan Stogumber gave a bitter laugh. He restarted the engine. 'Try Rising,' he said.

The light was improving in the sea direction but the rain still sheeted down drearily. A rather battered Morris Oxford Traveller, with a massive towing hitch, was parked at the Manor House behind Gently's Lotus. Lachlan Stogumber flicked the TR4 past it and braked sharply, raising a scatter of gravel. Gently got out. Lachlan Stogumber pulled the door shut, hesitated, then dropped the window a few inches.

'Have we finished with you?'

No.'

'I thought you'd been round all of us now.'

Gently shrugged and ran up the steps to the shelter of the Manor House porch. Lachlan Stogumber stared after him balefully, then raised the window, and sat, engine running. After some moments he revved the engine, circled, and drove back down the drive.

Gently rang; Redmayne opened to him. He greeted Gently with a doubtful smile.

'Come in,' he said. 'I would have fetched you, but the Wonderful Boy said he wanted words with you. I hope they were civil.'

Gently grunted and stepped past Redmayne into the hall. On a coatstand beside the door he noticed hanging a dripping storm-coat and a wet squash hat.

'Well, how was it?' Redmayne smiled. 'Did you find the lady forthcoming?'

Gently shook his head. Wet, recent footmarks were visible on the matting going up the hall.

'You'd better come into my den,' Redmayne smiled. 'You're looking draggy round the knees. You can dry off in front of the electric stove, and we can have a drink and some more chat.'

'Where's the office?' Gently said.

'Office . . . ?'

'Where James Stogumber does his estate-business.'

'Oh . . . that.' Redmayne's smile tightened. 'It's at the back, down the corridor. Did you want to see Jimmy?'

'I want to see him.'

'I think he's engaged just now . . .'

'All the same,' Gently said, beginning to head up the hall.

'Wait!' Redmayne moved swiftly in front of him. 'Perhaps I'd better announce you,' he said.

Without waiting for an answer he hastened along the corridor and tapped at the door on the right. He opened the door guardedly, put his head round it and said something in a low voice; then, still holding the door partly closed, he turned again to Gently.

'I did tell you the rain would bring us a visitor . . .'

Gently shouldered him aside. In the office, along with James Stogumber, sat the sprawling figure of Creke.

Stogumber was sitting at an old-fashioned desk, and Creke across from him in a stick-back chair. Both of them were staring at Gently but for the moment neither spoke. Gently glanced back at Redmayne. Redmayne grinned weakly then quietly withdrew down the corridor. Gently closed the door. He came into the room. He stood looking from one to other of the two occupants.

'Don't let me interrupt,' he said. 'Finish your business.'

James Stogumber drew back his head stiffly. 'Really,' he said. 'This is uncouth behaviour, Superintendent. Nobody invited you in here.'

'People rarely do,' Gently said. 'But in my line we have to make our own rules. So carry on as though I weren't here. I certainly shan't gossip about your estate business.'

Creke's dark eyes bored at him. 'Reckon we've finished.'

'We certainly have now,' Stogumber said.

'I believe you,' Gently said. 'But there wasn't much to discuss, was there? Not with all the cards being held on one side.'

Creke feinted a spit. 'Want to buy a horse?' he said.

'This . . . this is going too far,' Stogumber said, rising. 'You have no right to force your way in here, Superintendent, and your insinuations . . . they are contemptible.'

Gently shrugged. He looked at Creke. 'I'd say your horse was too pricy,' he said.

'Always was a good horse,' Creke said. 'You don't buy stallions like him for drink money.'

'What's he worth today?'

'About what he'll fetch.'

Gently nodded. 'Shall we say a year's rent?'

Stogumber came round the desk. 'I won't have this!' he said. 'Nat, I'm sorry, we'll finish our talk later.'

Creke pulled himself up. 'Don't worry, Jimmy,' he said. 'No snouty copper ever got change from me.' He leered at Gently. 'I'm not selling,' he said. 'You'd better take your custom to Clayfield.'

'Nat!' Stogumber said.

'I'm going,' Creke said. 'Don't let his nibs put anything across you.'

He swaggered out, closing the door noisily. Stogumber stood irresolute a moment, then returned to the desk. He dropped into the chair heavily, supporting himself by the desk, and sat breathing quickly and gazing at the desktop.

Gently sat himself in the stick-back chair.

'I've come from the Lodge,' he said. 'I've been talking to Marie.'

Stogumber drew himself straighter in his chair. He looked quickly at Gently, then away.

'A strange young woman,' Gently said. 'You don't quite know if you can believe what she tells you. Or even if she believes it herself. I'm inclined to think your daughter is a hysteric.'

'Her mother was one,' Stogumber said. 'Poor Stella. It ran in the family.'

'She believes she has a supernatural lover,' Gently said. 'One who is invisible.'

Stogumber let his veinous hand rise and fall on the desk.

'But of course, her lover's real enough,' Gently said. 'Real enough to be responsible for her condition. Real enough to write her amorous poems. Real enough to be hunted on the heath by Berney. He's flesh and blood, and he has a name – and I'm wondering just how many people know it.'

Stogumber groaned and closed his eyes.

'I think you'll be one of them,' Gently said. 'You must know who your daughter has been associating with, who came here often, was much in her company.'

Stogumber shook his head.

'Yes,' Gently said. 'And your son knows too. And your cousin. And Creke, naturally – he tumbled to it. And keeping Creke quiet will be expensive.'

'Oh, heavens, heavens!' Stogumber groaned.

'It can't go on,' Gently said. 'There are too many people in the secret. And we'll put on pressure. Someone'll crack.'

Stogumber's eyes opened wildly. His lips were trembling.

'So suppose you tell me,' Gently said.

'You want a . . . confession?' Stogumber stammered.

Gently stared at him, saying nothing.

Suddenly Stogumber's hand reached to his breast and he began to breathe heavily. The drooping flesh of his cheeks had lost colour, his eyes weren't focusing on Gently. He fumbled with a drawer. He brought out a brandy flask and tipped a little of the brandy into the metal cup. He swallowed it jerkily, leaning on the desk, his eyes watery and seeing nothing. Then he let the cup fall and sat huddled, his hand feeling for his breast again. His eyes found Gently. He shook his head.

'I'm old,' he said. 'A tired old man.' He made a little choking sound. 'I deserved better . . . I deserved a daughter with a little love for me.' He squeezed his eyes shut. Rheum wet his cheeks. 'Lachlan,' he said. 'Did you ask Lachlan?'

'Yes, I asked him,' Gently said.

'Aye . . . Lachlan wouldn't tell you,' Stogumber said. His lips fluttered, he bowed his head. 'The curse . . . it's on him too,' he said. 'Since he was a boy . . . you could always see it. He's the last, and he'll never marry.' He checked, nursing his breast. 'Leo . . . ?'

'I've questioned Mr Redmayne,' Gently said.

'Aye, aye,' Stogumber said. 'Leo sees all, but Leo says nothing. So it's the old man then . . . confess, and die. Well, it'd make an apt ending. Then you'll bury the business and go home . . . leave the Stogumbers to dree their weird.'

'Have you ever ridden that horse?' Gently said.

'On my better days,' Stogumber said. 'It's possible.'

'You had a reason to kill Berney?'

'Aye, to save the scandal. He would've come out with it. I couldn't allow that.'

'Who told you where to find him?' Gently said.

Stogumber's head shook. 'No more,' he said. 'We'll say I had word he would be on the heath, no matter from where. I could have known if I'd wished it.'

'One man could have told you,' Gently said.

'No,' Stogumber said. 'None of that. If I'm to confess, it's on my own terms. I'll not be party to involving others.'

He sat hugging his breast, his head tilted forward, the rheum trickling on his leaden cheeks. His words had been coming struggglingly, as though the weight of years was crushing his breath.

'I'm sorry,' Gently said. 'Truly sorry.'

He rose from his chair. Stogumber lifted his head. They looked at each other for several moments. Then Gently shrugged and turned away.

Redmayne was stationed in the corridor. His face was blank as Gently came out. But he managed to conjure a ghost of his smile as he led the detective back to the hall.

'So you didn't buy it.'

Gently halted to face him. 'Was I supposed to?' he asked.

Redmayne made a faint gesture. 'It sounded credible. The way old Jimmy was giving it to you.'

'You should know how credible it is.'

'Perhaps I should,' Redmayne said. 'And I can tell you one thing. I wasn't Jimmy's informant, which is what you were hinting at in there. I knew what I knew and I saw what I saw, but I was nowhere near the heath on Tuesday. So if Jimmy was tipped about Charlie's being there, you'll need to look a little further.'

'Of course,' Gently said. 'I was forgetting. You spent all Tuesday in the back woods.'

'In Stukey Woods,' Redmayne said. 'For the precise record. In praiseworthy search of *Orchis hircina*.'

'A faultless alibi.'

'Quite faultless. One I needn't prove and which you can't disprove. But keep me on your list, by all means. I've no interest in making it easy for you.'

He stood back from Gently, his eyes sulky, a petulant drag in his mouth; but almost immediately the expression switched, and he was his friendly self again.

'Look – it's no use! You have to act like a bastard, but I'm not going to act as though you really were one. What's happened here is damnable enough without you and I behaving like kids. Suppose we have that drink?'

Gently shook his head firmly. 'But if we're being such friends, you can give me some information.'

'Information about what?'

'About the Stogumber finances.'

Redmayne's smile went stiff.

'It's an angle I think we've neglected,' Gently said. 'I understand Charles Berney was a wealthy man. And when wealthy men are murdered it's always worth checking if there are less wealthy men who benefit. Yourself, for example.'

'I!'

'Or James Stogumber,' Gently shrugged. 'Or his son, with death duties hanging over him, which cannot be very long delayed.'

'But this is inconceivable!'

'Is it?' Gently said. 'Or is it the reason why Marie didn't marry her lover? Because he was poor? Because he had no prospects? Because Berney had the money that both of them wanted?'

'You don't know what you're saying!' Redmayne burst out. 'Jimmy's got money, and so has Lachlan. And as for death duties' – he pointed to the portraits – 'there's a Reynolds up there that can take care of them.'

'And you?' Gently said.

'Ask my broker.'

'I'd sooner you told me,' Gently said.

'All right,' Redmayne said. 'And welcome. I hold a block of Poseidon for a start.'

'Thank you,' Gently said. 'I may check that.'

'And then go to the devil,' Redmayne said. 'My God, you're dirty, you play it dirty. I was a fool to pretend you were a human being.'

He tramped to the door and threw it open, then stood by it, his eyes glinting. Gently went. He ignored Redmayne. Behind him he heard the door slam thunderously.

Outside, the rain was mizzling to a close and a greyish light was breaking over the heath. Gently got in the Lotus. He ran down a window, sat staring broodingly at the rain-dulled house. Then he took out Lachlan Stogumber's two manuscripts. He spread them both against the wheel. The second sonnet was undated,

151

though the ink appeared darker than the ink of the first.
It ran:

> Like Love's two only squires we sprang to arms
> And hotly reached for joy in one another,
> Compounding in a kiss all past alarms
> And seeking each in each his flames to smother;
>
> Our double rapture now was single fire
> That went about our bodies in fierce glee,
> Our two hands joined in one devout desire
> To take and tender melting ecstasy:
>
> And sudden we could speak our dear intending
> In free words, each such perfect partner finding,
> Owning our loveliest love, our longed-for
>   blending,
> With piercing thrill each one the other binding.
>
> A kiss, a touch, and open flew the door
> To all we wished, but only dreamed before.

Two sonnets; a similar style; but were they indeed
original drafts . . . ?

He glanced again at the house. Redmayne stood at a
window. His face was a blank paleness in the drained
light.

CHAPTER TWELVE

N<small>O MESSAGE WAITED</small> for him at the police station, and Docking and his team were still out. Gently tooled the Lotus back to the Royal William and parked it in the yard with the Capris and Vivas. But before going in to lunch he took a stroll in the High Street. In a peaked-gabled Georgian building he found Crampton's (Stationers). They were also booksellers in a small way, and after inspecting their windows, he went in.

'Do you have any books by Lachlan Stogumber?'

It was a safe bet: he was their local author. In addition, they carried a title by Leo Redmayne, *Fumariaceae of Great Britain*. It was priced at four guineas. Gently winced, but bought it, along with Lachlan Stogumber's *High On Ink*. The latter, clad in a brilliant psychedelic jacket, came more modestly at fifteen shillings.

He tucked the two books under his arm and sauntered in to lunch. Today the hotel dining-room was only half full and he had no difficulty in finding a secluded table. He laid the books on a chair and gave his order absent-mindedly. Somewhere, this morning, his finger had been close to it . . . why was it the coin hadn't dropped?

He ate mechanically, scarcely noticing when the waitress changed his plates. On the screen of his brain he was slowly playing back each word and detail of his several encounters. First there'd been Redmayne, then Lachlan Stogumber, then Redmayne again, then Mrs Berney; Lachlan Stogumber, trying to steer him off his sister, Redmayne, Creke and old Stogumber, and – once more! – Redmayne. And each one, except Creke, had tried to make a sale, had tried to steer Gently in a different direction . . . surely, if you put their various attempts together a common factor, the truth, ought to emerge?

Yet strangely, it didn't. The only common factor appeared to be an intent to confuse. Redmayne, Mrs Berney and Lachlan Stogumber had each in their way tried to hand him a *non sequitur*. Murder didn't follow: it was tragic inevitability, supernatural intervention, or a misread accident; while old Stogumber's unconvincing confession was a piece of desperation, aimed at the same end. They were covering: that was all. They sensed he was close, and they were trying to wrong-foot him. Perhaps the only significant point in the whole farrago was Lachlan Stogumber's assertion that a lover needn't have come into it . . .

Gently scrubbed his hands on a serviette and took the two books from the chair. They were published, he noticed, by the same publisher, and each bore the date of the current year. Also, they were each author-illustrated, Redmayne's with delicate colour plates, Lachlan Stogumber's with wavering line drawings,

154

some of which were slyly obscene. The poems were in the style of the *New Statesman* poem, patterns of words and printer's signs. Here and there were obscene phrases, but nothing that amounted to an articulate love-poem. Redmayne's prose, on the other hand, had a disciplined but easy clarity, and even though his matter was technical he had succeeded in conveying a touch of his personal charm. Gently grunted. Not much that corresponded! And the critical verdict was very clear. Grant the choice of these two for authorship of the sonnets, and the poll wouldn't go to Lachlan Stogumber.

He slapped the books together and accepted his coffee. Somewhere, he knew, he was missing something. There was a subtle factor about this case which he sensed intuitively, but which continued to elude him. Something behind there . . . He was standing on the edge of it, yet still couldn't drag it into view.

He gulped his coffee down impatiently. Meanwhile, you dealt with the facts you had!

In Docking's office the scene was domestic: they were making a late lunch of fish and chips. Four C.I.D. men with four packets, they sat around the desk tucking in. When Gently entered the only sounds were of rustling and champing, but then chairs scraped as the lunchers reluctantly got to their feet.

'Carry on,' Gently said. 'I've had mine.'

'Thanks, sir,' Docking said. 'We've been having a busy time of it. Did you have any luck with Redmayne, sir?'

'Nothing that would go on a charge sheet,' Gently said.

He strolled over to the window and filled his pipe. Behind him chairs scraped again and the champing recommenced. Across the M/T yard he could see shorn, sodden fields lying low and empty under a dull sky. The office, after the heat, felt almost chilly, and moisture had filmed on the window's metal frame. Two or three of the thunder-flies, which had been so lively, now climbed about the panes looking sickly and subdued. The storm had come and the storm had gone . . . what had it brought him, that he wasn't quite grasping?

He lit his pipe, shrugging, and sat himself on the table with the typewriter. Docking drained one of his brown bottles, balled his paper packet and wiped his hands on it.

'Well, sir,' he said. 'We've checked the list out.' Gently nodded. 'But no results.'

'I wouldn't quite say that, sir,' Docking said. 'There's one of them, Brightwell, who doesn't have an alibi.'

Gently considered. 'Didn't Mrs Berney mention a Brightwell?'

'Yes sir. Said she was talking to him at the party.'

'And he used to knock about with her?'

'Yes, sir, he admits that. But what he says is it never amounted to anything.'

Gently blew smoke. 'Let's have it,' he said.

'Well, sir, this Brightwell lives at Clayfield. He's an accountant who works with Livesy and Livesy, but on Tuesday he didn't come in. Says the party upset him or something, he had to keep running to the loo. And he was alone there Tuesday. He lives with his parents, but both of them were out most of the day.'

'Sounds promising,' Gently said. 'Is he a horseman?'

'Better than that, sir,' Docking said. 'He's a friend of the Risings. So like that, sir, he could have borrowed a horse, and the Risings wouldn't have let on to us.'

'Who did he go to the party with?'

Docking looked down his nose. 'That could be a snag, sir. He took a girl called Diane Stevenson, and according to him they've just got engaged.'

Gently formed a smoke-ring. 'Then we've lost our motive.'

'But the rest of it, sir! It fits like a glove.'

'When was he supposed to have knocked about with Mrs Berney?'

Docking humped his shoulders. 'Not lately, of course . . .'

That was Brightwell: and none of the others fitted like a glove or anything else. They consisted of three single young men, Stanford, Phillips and Greenhough, and a couple of newly-weds, Paston and D'Eath. The two latter had been accompanied by their wives and the three former by their girl friends. Each gave his place of work for alibi, and where these had been checked they stood up. Paston, D'Eath and Greenhough were horsemen and they patronized the Rising stable; D'Eath, who worked with Drury, the auctioneer, knew Creke by sight, but only as a customer at the livestock market. Stanford, junior partner at the local wine merchant's, and Greenhough, a surveyor, both admitted to being former admirers of Mrs Berney. But theirs was the same story as Tommy Brightwell's.

'Stanford thinks she was frigid, sir,' D.C. Waters contributed. 'I had a heart-to-heart chat with him down in the wine vaults. He fancied her a lot and she led him on a bit, but she always clamped down when he made a play. A tease, he says. She liked them to suffer. He reckons Berney was a hero, marrying her.'

'That's about what Greenhough said, sir,' Sergeant Bayfield said. 'He got to wondering whether the lady was a queer. She'd be all over a woman like Mrs Rising, but when it came to a bloke she'd got nothing for him.'

'But she used to go out with him?' Gently said.

'Oh yes sir, she'd knock around. But mostly her brother and Mr Redmayne came too, and it was just a show or dinner somewhere. Then he'd wangle to drive her home on his own and pull up at a quiet spot. Says she'd let him get worked up over her and then shy off. He never got anywhere.'

'Could be she is a queer,' Docking said. 'There's something about her, sir. She puts me off.'

'I don't know, sir,' D.C. Waters said slowly. 'She's quite a bird. And someone got there.'

'Perhaps it was bloody ignorance,' Bayfield said. 'She didn't know what it was all about. Then one time someone got to base, and the lady clicked, and made a grab for Berney.'

Gently drew a few times on his pipe. 'Unfortunately, this isn't what we're looking for,' he said. 'What we want is a man who Mrs Berney loves, not just a man who may have loved Mrs Berney. He belongs to her past. They must often have been together. In her eyes, he's a very remarkable man. For some reason, perhaps the simple one, she couldn't marry him. And he's horseman enough to manage Creke's stallion.' He puffed. 'I could add,' he said, 'that Mrs Berney describes him as being supernatural. But I think we should take a closer look at the mortals before we call in a clergyman.'

Docking's eyes rounded. 'She said that, sir?'

'She said he was invisible, and rode on the thunder.'

'Jesus,' Bayfield said. 'We're dealing with a nutter.'

Gently nodded. 'I'm not ruling that out.'

They thought about it silently for a space, each one keeping his eyes to himself. Bayfield, a shiny-faced man with a moustache, had his eyebrows hooked high, as though in indignant disbelief. Waters was absently cracking his fingers; Lubbock, an older man, had his eyes on his knees. Docking was frowning. He had a report sheet before him, and kept fretting at a corner in an irritating way. At last he looked up.

'Could *she* have done it, sir?' he said.

Now everyone else looked at Gently. Gently grinned at them through his smoke and added one or two fresh rings.

'I suppose it's possible,' he conceded.

'I mean, I know she's preggers, sir,' Docking said. 'But she's pretty limber with it, and it didn't stop her going riding on Sunday.'

'She wasn't riding Creke's stallion.'

'No, sir – but that doesn't mean she couldn't. Creke can ride it, and he did allow that Mrs Rising might, too. I'd say it was a case of getting to know the horse. I reckon Creke would know how to make him take to you. And Mrs Berney'd know Creke, and she's the sort who might have a go.' Docking's eyes glinted. 'In fact, it'd fit pretty well, sir,' he said. 'A man she might see a lot of – and Creke's wife can't be a lot of good to him.'

'By the centre,' Bayfield said. 'That's an angle, sir.'

'I reckon it fits all round,' Docking said. 'It never needed a man to ride that horse. That's where we've been wrong from the start.'

Gently jetted smoke. 'Follow it out,' he said.

'Yes, sir,' Docking said. 'Allowing she can ride the horse. Then all she has to do is to get Berney on the heath, and with him as jealous as sin it shouldn't have been difficult.'

'Creke didn't write that poem.'

'Didn't need to, sir. It could be the brother's, like they tell us. She just had to flash it around and make sure that Berney got an eyeful. Then he was set up. When he says he's going to town, she's pretty sure what he has in mind. So she lets him stew till the afternoon, then drives to the Home Farm and collects the horse.'

'What would make him keep watch on the heath?'

Docking hesitated. Bayfield weighed in.

'He'd know if she spent a lot of her time there, sir,' he said. 'And if he didn't, she could soon sell him the idea.'

'And him going to the valley?'

'Well, there,' Bayfield said. 'If you ask me it doesn't mean a thing. When she didn't turn up where he was staked out, he was bound to hunt around to see if he could spot her.'

Gently puffed. 'Then there's our horseman.'

'Coincidence, sir,' Docking urged. 'Could have been Rising every time. And you wouldn't expect him to admit it.'

Gently smiled benignly. A neat package! And it took care of some other things, too. Stogumber's halting confession, over-chivalrous when related to Redmayne, fell adroitly into place if it was intended to shield Marie. 'I deserved a better daughter . . .' Stogumber had almost sign-posted his motive. Yet, if Creke was Marie's lover, would he be so callous as to hold the threat of exposing her over Stogumber's head? Creke . . . Gently clicked his tongue.

'I doubt if Mrs Berney is a second Lady Chatterley.'

'Oh, I don't know, sir,' Docking said eagerly. 'You can't go a lot on that these days.'

'We're told she's frigid.'

'But that could be just the point, sir. She may have needed a bit of rough to get her going.'

'Plenty of dollies like that, sir,' Bayfield put in. 'Especially the uppity ones. They want a caveman.'

Gently swayed his shoulders. 'Maybe so! But do they make an idol of the caveman afterwards? Because that's what we have to assume with Mrs Berney, if we're to be left with a motive at all. Whoever it is, she worships him, and I can't see Creke filling her bill. The picture calls for a cultivated man, perhaps a man of distinction.'

'But she could still have done it, sir,' Bayfield said. 'It doesn't matter if Creke was her lover or not.'

'It means we'll need to think again,' Gently said. 'If the lover isn't Creke it blurs a nice, simple image.'

Docking stared glumly at his report sheet. 'It would come back to this, sir,' he said. 'Mr Redmayne.'

Gently nodded. 'But there's the problem. We know of no reason why he shouldn't have married her.'

'It wasn't money, sir?'

'Not unless he's a liar. And he's too clever for that.'

'A religious thing . . . ?'

161

'Do you know their religion?'

'They're not Catholics, sir,' Bayfield said. 'Or I would know it.'

Gently gestured. 'If we could find one reason, we could sink our teeth in Mr Redmayne. Until we can, he's laughing at us – and perhaps we're missing a better prospect.'

'A better prospect,' Docking repeated. The phone buzzed, and he grabbed it impatiently. He listened awhile, his face blank, then snapped, 'O.K.' and hung up. He looked at Gently. 'That was the desk,' he said. 'Rising's out there. He wants to talk to us.' He hesitated, his eyes calculating. 'Perhaps we were speaking of the devil,' he said.

Bayfield and the two D.C.s went out, taking with them the fish-and-chip papers and empty bottles. When Rising came in Gently had taken the desk chair and Docking was seated on his right. Rising halted to view this disposition.

'The Inquisition in session,' he sneered.

'You wanted to talk to us?' Gently said.

'Yuh,' Rising said. 'But like man to man.'

He spun the chair they'd put for him in front of the desk and sat down on it saddlewise, arms resting on the back. He was wearing breeches and a plaid shirt and a smart hacking jacket of soft tweed. He glanced quickly at Docking, then back to Gently.

'Right, we won't beat about the bush, sports,' he said. 'I've come to tell you to stop looking for Berney's woman, because that's not what this kick-up's about.'

Docking gazed at him. 'You've come to tell us that?'

'True,' Rising said. 'That's the message. I could've told you yesterday, but I had reasons. So now I've come to tell you today.'

Docking snorted. 'We know that,' he said.

Rising's eyes jumped to him. 'You know it?' he said.

'We're not exactly stupid round here,' Docking said. 'If that's the lot, you're wasting our time.'

Rising's stare hardened. 'So if you know it,' he said, 'what games were you playing out at my place yesterday?'

'That's our business,' Docking snapped. 'We don't know anything that puts you in the clear.'

Rising stared a moment longer, then he jumped to his feet. 'You're right, sport, I'm wasting your time,' he said. 'I should've known better than to come round here – you won't catch me on that kick again.'

'Whoa!' Gently said. 'Sit down, Mr Rising.'

'I don't have time to waste either,' Rising said.

'Sit down,' Gently said. 'There is something you can tell us. What were your reasons for not speaking up yesterday?'

Rising glared at him, his hands still on the chair-back. Reluctantly, he sank back on the chair. 'They're about what you might think,' he said. 'Loyalty to friends. Or is that something the coppers don't know about?'

'Which friends?' Gently said.

'Mrs Berney. I didn't want to drop her in the cart.'

'But today you're telling us?'

'Too right I am. And don't think I'm feeling a hero, either.' He scowled at the desk. 'It's my skin,' he said. 'You'd got me backed into a corner. No effing alibi, a damn fat motive, and even Jill in the bag, too. Loyalty's a bloody fine thing, sport, but there's a time and place for everything.'

'So you knew what was happening between the Berneys.'

Rising sank his head. 'I did by Monday.'

'Something at the party?'

'Yeah, the party. What happened after it, anyway.'

'What did happen after it?'

Rising wagged his head. 'The sheilas put their coats in Charlie's office. We were in there last, when the others had gone, me helping Jill get into her coat. Then we heard Marie give a yelp. We shot out into the hall. She came blazing past us and up the stairs. She'd got a letter in her hand.'

'A letter?' Gently said.

'Looked like one to me,' Rising said. 'And there was Charlie down the hall with a face like frozen death. Properly shook me, Charlie did. Looked as though he'd just run into Medusa. I went up and said something to him, but he never spoke a word.'

'And from this you deduced Marie was being unfaithful.'

'Deduced is right,' Rising said. 'Charlie was hit clean out of the ground. I never saw a bloke so chilled-off as he was.'

Gently gave a little shrug. 'Strange,' he said.

'Huh?' Rising said. 'What's strange?'

'Berney being so upset. When he'd known for some time that his wife did have a lover.'

'Yeah, but now he knew who,' Rising said. 'He'd read the letter. That was the bit that was knocking Charlie.'

'The letter would have told him?'

'Sure,' Rising said. 'It had the bloke's signature. I saw it.'

'Who?' Gently said.

Rising rocked his chair back, his narrowed eyes glinting at Gently. 'Don't get me wrong, sport,' he said. 'I didn't read the letter. I only caught sight of it whipping past me. But it was headed up and signed, I can give you that straight. And it had been folded up small. There were a lot of creases in it.'

'Handwritten or typed?'

'Handwritten.'

'How much writing?'

Rising weaved his head. 'I didn't have time to get my rule out,' he said. 'It was just a sheet of notepaper, pretty well written over.'

Gently took the Lachlan Stogumber manuscripts from his wallet and held one leaf up, keeping it distant from Rising.

'About this much?'

Rising peered at it keenly. 'Give or take some lines. It was a larger sheet.'

'Similar handwriting?'

'Break it down,' Rising said. 'All I can tell you was it wasn't typed.'

'What about the ink?'

'It was ink,' Rising said. 'Not red, not green. Just effing ink.'

Gently put the leaf away. 'All the same, you saw plenty – just coming out of the study, with Mrs Berney running by you.'

Rising's eyes slitted. 'I saw what I saw. I shan't lose any sleep if you don't believe me.'

'Of course, it lets you out. It wasn't your letter.'

Rising eased off the chair. 'You through?' he said.

'Just a last question,' Gently said. 'Who slipped it to her?'

'Get stuffed,' Rising said. He headed for the door. 'Wait,' Gently said.

Rising halted.

'Tell me which of the guests left just before you.'

Rising turned with a leer. 'Her brother and Leo. And they don't write letters – they use the phone.'

He slammed out. Gently sat silent, his arms leaning on the desk. Docking was staring viciously after Rising. He had spots of colour in his cheeks.

'I suppose we can't tie that joker in, sir?'

Gently shook his head. 'Not on what we've got.'

'All the same, I'll fix him with something, sir. The way he drives it shouldn't take long.'

Gently shrugged and struck a match for his pipe. 'It doesn't fit,' he said. 'The signed letter. If Berney knew his wife's lover's identity, why did he set watch for him the next day?'

'Perhaps he wanted more proof, sir.'

'Proof of what?'

'Well – like seeing it with his own eyes. Maybe he had a divorce in mind. Or maybe he aimed to give the bloke a hiding.'

Gently brooded over his pipe. 'There's another alternative. Whatever was in the letter seems to have been a great shock. He was acting almost as though he couldn't believe it, as though the knowledge had overwhelmed him. Yet he knew that his wife had a lover, and he must have suspected the same people we suspect. The name on the letter only confirmed a suspicion . . . so what was it knocked him into a heap?'

'We only have Rising's word for it, sir,' Docking said.

'Why should Rising mislead us about that?'

'It sort of puts him in the clear, sir, if he's the man. He's telling us Berney was upset about someone else.'

'But if he isn't the man?'

'Then Redmayne is, sir. And I reckon that'd be enough to knock Berney cold. And Rising did say Redmayne left just ahead of him, which was likely when the letter was passed.'

Gently nodded. 'Only Redmayne is fireproof.'

'That's as far as we know, sir,' Docking urged. 'If we can once prove otherwise we'll have him.'

Gently hunched his shoulders, puffing.

The telephone rang. Docking took it. He listened for a moment, then covered the mouthpiece.

'It's for you sir . . . Mrs Berney.'

Gently stared, took the instrument, held it aslant.

'Is that you, Superintendent?' said Mrs Berney's voice. 'I've been doing some thinking since your visit, Superintendent. I've come to the conclusion that you're so hopelessly at sea that it's time I gave you a little assistance. Are you listening?'

'I'm listening,' Gently said.

'I was sure you would be,' Mrs Berney said. 'Between ourselves you are stumped, aren't you? And really I'm the only person who can help you.'

'You and one other,' Gently said.

Mrs Berney's laughter came cuttingly. 'So I'm being

rather generous, don't you think – coming to the aid of a benighted policeman?'

'What have you to tell me, Mrs Berney.'

'Nothing,' she said. 'But I've something to show you. Something you want to see very much, and which you'll never see unless I do show you. Would you like me to show you?'

Gently said nothing.

'Oh, but of course you would,' Mrs Berney said. 'And I'm going to show only you, Superintendent, because the local peasants wouldn't understand. So you must meet me in half an hour at the survey point on the heath. Is that clear? In half an hour. Be kind enough not to keep me waiting.'

'I can come to your house,' Gently said.

'You can, but you won't,' she said. 'I shall wait for you fifteen minutes at the survey point. After that, the deal is off.'

CHAPTER THIRTEEN

Gently hung up. His eyes met Docking's. The local man was wonderingly shaking his head.

'That bitch is a case,' he said. 'A proper case. A mental home is where she'll end up.'

'How long since Rising left here?' Gently said.

Docking's eyes flickered. 'You think there's a connection?'

'I think he had time to get to a call-box – and I don't want to miss a trick at this stage.'

Docking's hand reached for the phone, but Gently pushed the hand aside.

'Hold it! If Mr Rising is playing games, this isn't the time to interfere.'

'But this could be a trap, sir.'

'It could,' Gently said. 'And we won't find out by putting stickers on Rising. So we'll just let him go about his business, while I keep my assignation with the lady.'

'But sir – if it's something crazy!'

Gently pulled a face. 'Unlikely,' he said. 'More probably they've cooked up some little trick which they hope will mystify our small intelligence.' He tapped out his pipe in Docking's ashtray. 'But you can post a couple of cars,' he said. He blew through his pipe. 'And yourself, with glasses. That should take care of the comic element.'

'But . . . nobody goes with you, sir?'

'Nobody. The lady asked to see me alone.'

Docking stared at him with unhappy eyes. He was a man of forty: he looked older.

The rain had ceased, but a smoking mist had followed it in from the sea – thin, straying stuff with more wetness than apparent substance. It poured about in coombes and declivities but didn't obscure the plane of the heath, which lifted steamily towards a slate sky, its dimmed acres smudgy and purplish.

As he passed the great cleft that split the cliff of the plateau, Gently glanced automatically to his right. Mist was hanging over the apron of sea and clinging about the trees of the village. The tractor which had clicked about the fields yesterday now stood sheeted and still in a corner. Nothing was moving down there either – rained off! The storm had closed play.

He bumped round a bend in the track; the survey point came into view. A flaming figure in a red raincoat, Mrs Berney was leaning nonchalantly against her parked Vitesse. She wore no hat, and her blonde hair lifted lightly in a faint breeze. She stood coolly watching the approach of the Lotus, a cigarette between her fingers.

Gently trundled his car up to the Vitesse, parked and got out. Mrs Berney flashed him a scathing look and tossed her cigarette into the bushes.

'You're late,' she said. She glanced at her wristwatch, a tiny movement on a jewelled bracelet. 'You've kept me waiting five minutes. Were you scared of me or something?'

'Should I be scared?'

She flicked her hair. 'I could be carrying a gun or a knife, couldn't I? And you must be feeling that you have become a little over-intimate with my affairs. But perhaps you're armed.'

Gently shook his head.

'Then you'll be a grand master of unarmed combat.'

'Perhaps,' Gently said. 'Also, I have colleagues who know where I am and who I'm with.'

'Colleagues,' she sniffed. 'You've none within a mile – I know that, because I've been watching. You're alone here with me, and nobody in sight, so if I had a gun you'd be a dead man.'

'Well,' Gently said. 'Do you have a gun?'

She stared at him tauntingly, her head drawn back. 'You don't know, do you?' she said. 'And we'll keep it that way. Because one thing is certain – you can't search me.'

'Show me your handbag.'

Mrs Berney laughed, reached into the Vitesse and threw him a handbag. It was a small, expensive, lizard-skin bag, and it contained only money, driving-licence and keys. He handed it back. She dropped it in the car. Her movements moulded the lightweight raincoat to her figure. If she was carrying a weapon it wasn't apparent: the raincoat wrapped her body smoothly.

'Now . . . if you'll get in my car we can talk.'

'Talk!' Her hair swept across her shoulders. 'We've nothing to talk about. I made it abundantly clear that the purpose of this meeting was to show you something.'

'Then you can show it to me.'

'But not in the car.'

'Why not in the car, Mrs Berney?'

'Because,' she said, 'it wouldn't go in the car. It's out over there – where they found Charlie.'

Gently hesitated. 'It's something on the heath?'

'Exactly,' she said. 'That's why we're here.'

'But the heath has been searched. We used men with dogs.'

'But this you didn't find,' she said. 'Not this.'

Gently was silent. Mrs Berney was gazing at him with a gleam in her handsome eyes. She was lounging against the car casually, yet there was a hint of alertness in her easy stance. Gently's eyes strayed to the mist-laden heath. Nothing stirred, there was no sound. A long way off, almost blanked out by mist, was the thicket where Docking would now be stationed with his glasses. Mrs Berney laughed softly.

'We're quite alone,' she said. 'That's the essence of the contract. But of course, if you're scared you can get back in your car, and never know the secret I nearly showed you. Do you want to do that?'

'You could tell me,' Gently said.

'Oh yes,' she said. 'But I won't. And in any case you'd have to verify what I told you, so that wouldn't be much gain, would it? Well . . . are you coming?'

Gently hunched a shoulder. 'Perhaps you'd like to lead,' he said.

She laughed, swinging forward off the Vitesse.

'Of course. I'm the one who knows where we're going.'

She set off on a line along the rim of the plateau, not heading directly for the place of the tragedy. She walked springily, showing that same curious detachment from the burden of her belly. It wasn't part of her; she didn't acknowledge it. It was an alien thing which she took in her stride. Beneath the drape of the raincoat it scarcely noticed, except when a vigorous movement briefly shaped it. She turned to watch Gently plodding after her.

'Don't let me go too fast, will you?' she said. 'I'm not used to keeping pace with cockney policemen, and I should hate to get you puffed.'

'Should you be so active?' Gently said.

'Oh yes. My doctor recommends it. And you have to remember that I'm a special case – I'm carrying a foetus for a demon lover.'

'That, of course, must make a difference.'

Mrs Berney laughed harshly. 'All the difference. Witches don't expect pain or inconvenience when they're brooding a cub for the Prince of Darkness. It doesn't affect me.

'In fact . . . it's almost unreal.'

'Unreal.' She checked her stride to stare at him. She laughed again. 'That's a marvellous theory! You must be really baffled, to come up with that. Would you like me to strip?'

'Unreal to you . . . you're pregnant, but you haven't become a mother.'

'You're sure you don't think my lump is a fake.'

'I think you don't think of yourself in that way.'

Mrs Berney paused, her eyes fierce. 'I like it the other way best,' she said. 'It's more dramatic. A strapped-on lump. And me really a les, with a female lover. Wouldn't Jill Rising fit?'

'Jill Rising?' Gently said.

'Yes. Jill Rising can handle a horse.'

'Both the Risings can handle horses,' Gently said.

'But Jill Rising is best. And Jill does fancy me.'

Gently shook his head. 'Your pregnancy is a fact. Only . . . somehow . . . it means something different to you.'

Mrs Berney's eyes stabbed at him. 'You're dangerous,' she said. 'Yes, you're dangerous.'

She stalked on. The direction she'd taken had put them out of sight of Docking's glasses. Below them, seaward, were now and then glimpses of the coast road leading from Clayfield. An occasional car crept along the road, which at this point made a curve towards the heath. Leftwards the sodden heath was featureless except for its smoking vales and shallows.

'Don't think I underrate you,' Mrs Berney snapped. 'On the contrary, I had you sized up from the beginning. I knew we wouldn't bamboozle you about Charlie, and I didn't really try. It was too obvious. When Charlie had a woman he could scarcely be bothered to cover his tracks. Ergo, he was playing the fool for some other reason, and that was staring you in the face.'

'It didn't need me to spot it,' Gently said.

'Oh, I think it did,' Mrs Berney sneered. 'The locals were too besotted with Charlie's record. It called for your eager, penetrating eye. And now you have it, and you've begun to think about it, which Inspector Docking would hardly do. No, I didn't under-rate you. Your fumbling fingers are digging down there.'

'You couldn't marry him,' Gently said.

Her burning eyes looked into his. 'You're probing, guessing,' she said. 'You're not there yet. And you'll get small help out of me.'

'You couldn't marry him, so you married Berney.'

'Berney was any woman's fool.'

'But you needed Berney. There was a reason.'

'And here it is – my stomach.' She gave a wild laugh. 'You're forgetting,' she said. 'The Stogumber family pride is in my keeping. Fathering a bastard is no great matter when the pride of the Stogumbers is at stake.'

'And was it at stake?'

'Oh, very much so.' She sent her long hair twirling.

'How much?' Gently said.

'Too much. Poor Charlie really never had a chance.'

She came to a halt at a small, round hillock, grown about at the foot with stunted gorse; she mounted it, standing in the precise centre, an arresting figure in her bright raincoat.

'Here's a witch's circle,' she said. 'Would you like me to raise Beelzebub? He prefers to come at midnight, but I have some spells which he daren't disobey.'

Gently shrugged. 'Is this what we've come for?'

'No.' She glanced fleetingly at the heath. 'What we've come for is in the valley. But we have to approach it from the right direction.'

'So shall we do that.'

'When I'm ready.'

She remained for several moments standing on the hillock; then slowly she raised and lowered her arms, as though in an act of supplication. She came down.

'I'm ready now. I felt it was right to propitiate the spirits.'

'Would one of the spirits be Old Shanks?'

She stared at him stonily and led into the heath.

The line now departed from the rim and took them on a course diagonal to it. As far as Gently could judge it was aiming at the valley, but the featureless heath offered no landmark. They were crossing a sweep of trackless heather-bush. Distantly ahead were low, mist-laden ridges. They were working back a little on the way they'd come, but the cars and the survey point were well out of sight. Soon, he was aware, his sense of direction would be at fault, and he would be depending entirely on Mrs Berney's guidance.

'Naturally . . . you've known this heath all your life.'

She gave her soft laugh. 'Are you worried I shall lose you?'

'Your family too. They all grew up here.'

'Every Stogumber,' she said. 'For centuries.'

'Your father and brother.'

Mrs Berney said nothing.

'And your father's cousin.'

She tossed her head.

'But your husband,' Gently said. 'He was an odd man out.'

Her laugh was harder. 'Charlie didn't love the heath.'

'An odd man out,' Gently said. 'He didn't belong to

176

the Stogumber clan. When the chips were down, Charlie was expendable. And you spent him to give your bastard a name. Or . . . was that the reason?'

She turned on him savagely. 'Perhaps you'd better stop your prying there! The Stogumber secrets are dangerous to know, even for a Superintendent from Scotland Yard.'

'But Berney discovered them.'

'He was a fool. He had to be prying, just like you.'

'And it wasn't merely that you had a lover.'

'It was too much for a fool – and he paid the penalty!'

'Too much for him to stand.'

Mrs Berney loomed close to him, her breath coming in jerky gasps. Her eyes were distended and her mouth squared, her long fingers hooked and working.

'You're not God,' she said. 'You're another little man. And little men have never been a match for me. On this heath I command Lucifer and bring him riding on the storms. Yes, Charlie learned secrets, fatal secrets, secrets that turned his foolish brain. And the madness brought him on the heath, and I conjured my demon lover to meet him. And what can you do about that?' She thrust her face close to Gently's. 'Nothing! Unless I myself were to conjure my love into your arms.'

'Does your demon lover write letters?'

'Letters! Ha!' She pulled away from him.

'And does he sometimes borrow a horse – when the storms, of course, are not convenient?'

'Little man,' she said. 'Remember where you are and who you're with.'

'I think I'm with a phoney,' Gently said. 'And a pretty obvious one at that.'

Mrs Berney's hand flew up, the fingers crooked, and her eyes flared destruction.

'Don't,' Gently said. 'You couldn't do it. And it wouldn't be clever to try.'

'You peasant,' she spat. 'You bloody peasant!'

'Yes,' Gently said. 'The Stogumber curse.'

'May it light on you, may it, may it!'

'In the meantime,' Gently said, 'put down your hand.'

Her eyes savaged him, but abruptly she dropped her hand to her side.

'You're probably right,' she said. 'You're not worth it. My nails are too good for your ugly face.' She gave a shudder. 'Let's get this over – before I'm sick, or have a miscarriage.'

Gently nodded. 'Whatever it might be.'

She tossed her head furiously and strode on.

They were passing the ridges on their right and keeping to the level plains of heather. A very slight incline suggested to Gently that now they were working towards the track. Somewhere across there, among the vapoury bushes, Docking perhaps was picking them up again – relieved, no doubt, to see Gently returning in the same shape as he went. But if Docking was there, he was well concealed. The wrack-blurred heathscape stretched emptily as ever. From the coombes below the ridges mist crawled out serpent-like, urged up from the lower level by a feeble breeze.

'Nearly there now,' Mrs Berney said. 'You won't need your patience much longer, policeman. You want to understand and you shall understand – but don't blame me if it isn't any use to you.'

'Everything is of use to me,' Gently said quietly.

Mrs Berney's laughter was hoarse. 'You have your philosophy, policeman,' she said. 'But what you'll see now is a little outside it. Stand here.'

She pointed to a burn of gravel which lay naked and glimmering amongst the heather. It was roughly circular, and its centre was marked by a mat of black flints.

'Stand on that.' She moved Gently on to it, then turned him to face towards the ridges. Once again he felt surprise at finding himself looking into the valley where the body had been found. 'Now stay still. Don't move from the centre. Just keep facing down the valley. Then, when I lift the veil, you'll be able to see what you've come to see.'

She placed her feet on the flints beside his, turned, and began pacing a line to his left. Almost compulsively, he found himself counting each of her precisely measured steps. At seventy-seven she reached a stony mound that lifted a little above the heather. At ninety-nine she reached the summit, halted, and turned to face the valley. She raised her arms. She began to incant. At the distance he couldn't hear the words. When she'd finished, she crossed her arms seven times, then sank them slowly, with fingers extended.

'Now policeman – listen! Can you hear him?'

She stood with arms pressed back, her face raised and intent. And Gently heard it: from down the valley, a dull beat, like a muffled drum.

It came out of the mist, and it was black, a black rider on a black horse – and it was huge, seeming above life-size as it cantered majestically up the valley. The

179

rider sat straight, his hands low, his head and face a blotted blank. Man and horse, they moved together in an unhurried, rhythmic progress.

'Do you see him?' Mrs Berney cried. 'Do you see my lover coming, mortal?' She burst into a peal of hysterical laughter, her hands clasping about her belly. 'You wanted to meet him – now he's here! What have you to say to him? How will you greet him?' She swayed from side to side: her laughter sounded like agony.

Hoof clashed on stone and thudded on heather. Involuntarily, Gently turned to run. But there was no cover. The spot where she'd brought him was a bare heather flat, dotted only with dwarf gorses. Distantly he could see the crowns of trees peeping over the big crevasse – too far off, but there was nothing else: he began to sprint in that direction.

'Run, run policeman!'

Mrs Berney was running too. From the corner of his eye he could see her red raincoat trailing along on a parallel course. The ponderous rhythm behind him didn't quicken but insensibly, regularly, drew closer, the hoofbeats gaining in articulation, the rough breathing of the stallion beginning to sound over them. Another hundred, hundred and twenty yards . . .

Then, away to his right, he heard a shout. Two figures, one of whom he recognized as Docking, were racing jerkily across the heather towards him. But they were quarter of a mile off, and what could they do? As though conscious of this, they had come to a standstill. But almost immediately Gently heard a vicious whine, followed by a report, and a commotion behind him.

Docking had a rifle!

Panting, Gently wheeled about. The stallion and its rider were only fifty yards behind him. It hadn't been hit, but it was rearing and struggling, its white-rimmed eyes starting from their sockets.

'Get him – get him!' Mrs Berney was screaming. 'The others don't matter, but you must get him!'

The rider climbed high in his stirrups above the stallion, driving him down, driving him forwards.

Gently rushed on. Another bullet split air. This time he didn't wait to see the effect. Before him the track was snaking through the heather-bush and beyond the track opened the gulf of the crevasse. His feet banged stones and snagged in the heather. A clamp seemed screwed across his lungs. The hoofbeats were gaining on him much too fast, were increasing tempo, were bearing in on him. He stumbled over the track. There were still ten yards. Hooves clattered on the track straight behind him. A bullet whanged by his head, he tripped, sprawled, rolled, was plunging suddenly into wet, rasping bracken. Hooves flailed above him: the stallion neighed. There was darkness, then light, then a dragging silence. Then, some way below, he heard a crashing thud, followed by the spine-chilling screams of the stallion.

He clawed out of the bracken. Forty feet beneath him the stallion was pawing at the slope with desperate forefeet. Its hind-quarters were paralysed, and it was sliding, shrieking, farther and farther down the incline. Some yards above it lay the black-clad rider, blood rippling through his stocking mask. His head looked flattened, his trunk misshaped; one arm was bent in the wrong place.

Gasping painfully, legs trembling, Gently began lowering himself towards the body; but then the red-clad figure of Mrs Berney darted over the top and came thrusting past him.

'No. No. Oh no – no!'

She tumbled and fought through the clinging bracken. Sobbing, wailing, she threw herself on the body, grabbing the mangled trunk to her, nuzzling the bloody head.

Gently staggered down beside her. He took hold of the stocking mask and wrenched. For a second he stared without recognition at the crushed and bloodstained features the mask had hidden. Then he knew. The hair was auburn. He was looking at Lachlan Stogumber. The wailing woman clutching the body was bathing her face in her brother's blood.

CHAPTER FOURTEEN

DOCKING SHOT THE stallion.

He had taken alarm when he'd seen Gently leave the cars with Mrs Berney. He'd sent a Panda to Creke's stable, and finding it empty, had asked for a gun.

The stallion wasn't easy to shoot. Though crippled, it had gone for Docking with its teeth. He'd shot it at last, blasting out one of the eyes, and was violently sick directly afterwards. Now he stood around looking dazed and wretched while the ambulance men fetched up Lachlan Stogumber's body.

'But what are we going to do about her . . . ?'

Docking's eyes kept straying to Mrs Berney. Mrs Berney was sitting slumped in the back of the car with a policewoman at her side. They'd had to use force to get her off the body and for a while she'd seemed to go out of her mind; then the hysteria had collapsed suddenly and she'd fallen into a staring-eyed stupor.

Gently looked blankly towards the car. 'She's disturbed . . . we'd better take her home.'

'You mean to the Lodge?'

'No – the Manor. There's a housekeeper there who may understand her.'

'But . . . there'll have to be charges?'

Gently's shoulder twitched. 'That's something we can talk about later. Just now we're taking her to the Manor. I've still some business to finish there.'

It was raining again, a soft rain, sheeting in quietly from the sea. Gently's Lotus led the small cavalcade that bumbled down the track to the road. He drove slowly. Docking rode with him. At the junction in the grove they parted with the ambulance. Creke, a sack draped round his shoulders, was waiting at his lane's end; he waved them to stop, but Gently ignored him. They reached the Manor. A Panda car was parked there. The driver was standing at the foot of the steps. On the steps stood Stogumber, bare-headed in the rain, his face a wet smudge against the gloom of the doorway. They parked and got out. The second car parked. The policewoman handed out Mrs Berney. Stogumber came down the steps; his body was trembling, his gnarled hands on the flutter.

'Marie . . .'

Mrs Berney stared through him. Her eyes were icy, her mouth sagged.

'Marie. Marie. My daughter . . .'

She drew a sudden, fierce breath and turned aside.

Stogumber rocked a little. He looked for Gently. 'Please,' he said. 'Where have you taken him?'

'To the mortuary.'

'He mustn't come . . . here?'

'I don't think you'd want that,' Gently said.

They went into the hall. Redmayne was waiting

there. Mrs Berney stalked past him and flopped on a chair. She sat hugging her belly and gazing at the rush matting, her lips very thin and skewed to the side. Stogumber shambled up near her, his hands still fluttering, his lips framing words he didn't speak. Tears, it may have been of rheum, were dribbling down his grey cheeks.

Gently halted by Redmayne. 'And you . . . you warned nobody.'

Redmayne was pale, his eyes bright. He made a resigned motion with his hand. 'Jimmy probably guessed . . . in the end.'

'But you could have told him. Long since.'

'It wouldn't have helped.'

'It would have helped Berney.'

'Charlie . . .' Redmayne shook his head. 'He bought it, you know . . . with his own weakness.'

'His weakness – and your silence.'

Redmayne hunched, his head sinking. 'They were kin,' he said. 'Stogumber kin. How could you expect me to come out with it?'

Mrs Berney gave a crowing laugh. 'My God, you hypocrites,' she said. 'Furtive, craven, beastly hypocrites. My love was noble. Let the world know!'

'Hush, Marie, hush,' Redmayne said.

'I won't be hushed,' Mrs Berney said. She rose from the chair to stand challengingly, head drawn back, eyes glittering. 'We dared. Our love was immortal. He was a king and I a queen. Ours was the love of royal people – of Pharaohs, emperors. Of the gods.'

'Be quiet, be quiet,' Redmayne said.

'Why?' she said. 'What should I be afraid of? The peasant laws are for peasant people, they can never touch

185

such ones as us. Here.' She felt in her bosom and pulled out a piece of folded paper. 'Here it is – Charlie Berney's death warrant. He looked on this and had to die.'

She threw it on the matting at Gently's feet. Gently picked it up and unfolded it. Written on it was the first sonnet, in Lachlan Stogumber's hand, headed: *To My Sister-mistress*, and signed: *Lachlan Rex*.

'He was doomed,' Mrs Berney said. 'He read the riddle and it was death to him. We knew what he'd do, where he would go. It was I who decreed that Charlie should die.'

'Marie – no!' Redmayne exclaimed.

'Yes – I, I!' Mrs Berney said. 'Tell the world – do you think I care? There's nothing left now in this place of graves.'

A grasping groan came from Stogumber. He shuffled a step forward to confront his daughter. His mouth hung open, his eyes were searching, his wandering hands shook like leaves.

'Marie . . .'

It ended in a choking sound, rattling deep in his throat. Then he fell, going down quickly. He landed lumpingly on his back on the matting.

'Get her out of here!' Gently snapped. 'Take her back to the car.'

'Die, old man!' Mrs Berney screamed. 'Don't let the peasants drag you back!'

She was grabbed by Docking and the policewoman and hustled, laughing crazily, out of the hall. Redmayne had dropped beside his cousin. He was supporting Stogumber's lolling head on his arm. Gently knelt, took Stogumber's wrist.

'I think he's gone,' Redmayne whispered. 'My God . . . she's killed him too. Poor Jimmy. Poor old Jimmy.'

There was no pulse. Gently released the wrist. Stogumber's cheeks were drained and pallid. The jaw sagged, and below sunken lids the eyes showed rolled and white. He was dead.

'Oh heavens,' Redmayne whispered.

Very tenderly, he lowered Stogumber's head. He took the dead man's hand and squeezed it till his own knuckles went pale.

The outer door opened. Docking had come back. One of his hands was streaming blood. He stood gazing at them, his face working, his eyes clownish in their aghastness.

Gently jumped up. Docking's lips jigged.

'That bitch . . . she had a knife!'

'A knife!'

'I tried to stop her . . .'

Blood from his hand was pattering on the rushes.

Norwich, 1969–70.